THE DAMNED

CLASSIC MONSTERS

MERCEDES M. YARDLEY   TIM WAGGONER

JEFF STRAND   MATHEW KAUFMAN   JEFF DEPEW

LANCE TAUBOLD   LEAH SNOW

Dumblebee

For my dogs. If it wasn't for you my feet would have been too cold to write this book. On the other hand, the room wouldn't have smelled like farts. Thanks, Nyx...

CONTENTS

ACKNOWLEDGMENTS

I would like to thank Mercedes M. Yardley. This book wouldn't have been successful without you. I would also like to thank F. Paul Wilson for his wisdom on writing. Jeff Strand, Tim Waggoner, and Stephen King, thank you for your books on writing that answered so many questions. And Brandon Sanderson, for your willingness to share your knowledge and your honesty in doing so.

"If you battle monsters, you don't always become a monster. But you aren't entirely human anymore, either."

— JONATHAN MABERRY

SUM OF HER PARTS

MERCEDES M. YARDLEY

Light. Pain. Noise, too much and too loud. She tried to scream, but there was something wrong with her mouth, with her throat, and she growled instead.

Where? She wanted to say. *How?*

She had been walking, or running, or lying in a field. She had been hard at work at the anvil, or laughing with her lover, or crying over her spouse's infidelity.

Playing with toys, a wolf made of wood.

Skinning a rabbit for dinner.

She moaned again, head splitting, memories fragmenting, and tried to bring her hand to her brow.

She couldn't move.

"She's alive!" a man shouted beside her. She cringed and tried to squirm away. "It worked, dear God, it worked." She blinked her eyes but couldn't see. Dark, like a tunnel. Dark, like a grave.

"Don't worry, darling," the man said gently. A storm moved behind him. She heard thunder, sensed wind. The hair on her arms stood tall, warning her of lightning.

"My name is Doctor Frankenstein," the man said, and

gently unwound gauze from her face. "Your name is Marieke. Can you see me?"

His words pattered like rain. She blinked and saw a silhouette. A shadow. A man. She tried to focus on his face.

"Good, good," he said, and grinned. His teeth were white and sharp. She bared her own teeth in response.

"Wonderful. And your hands?"

He continued to pull at the bandages wrapped around her arms. She peered down, seeing gauze, seeing wounds, seeing that things were put together *wrong,* put together *not right.* She was too tall, her feet farther away from her than they had ever been. She couldn't touch them with her fingers if she tried. She was tied to a metal table. Hard. Uncomfortable.

Lightning zapped overhead. Thunder crashed. The ceiling was broken stone, exposed to the elements. More storm, more sound.

Scary.

"Don't struggle, darling," the doctor said, but something in his eyes made her cower, made her want to fight, and the pain in her head ratcheted up inch by inch by inch.

"Marieke," he said, but she was screaming, the sound tearing from her ruined throat, her lips parted wide and her mouth turning into a black hole.

She was being chased. She was being beaten. By the robbers. The police. Her parents. Her brother.

Memories that she didn't know. Reactions she couldn't control. Her feet pedaled in the air and her fingers curved into claws.

"Marieke!"

Pain. Hurt. Blows that landed on her head, her legs, her torso. She remembered curling up under the kitchen sink. She remembered beating her wife until her beautiful hair ran red. She swung her cleaver in the butcher's shop. She snuffled against her lover's hair while she slept.

Thoughts, sounds, memories, lifetimes. They weren't hers. She didn't remember herself, didn't remember her childhood, and certainly didn't remember this strange Marieke name this strange doctor kept shouting at her.

The commotion. Too much, too frightening. She screamed back, shrieking, letting the terror and rage bubble up like blood. *This is wrong,* she howled. *Something is wrong!* But the words stayed somewhere deep in her chest. They swirled around in lungs that didn't feel familiar and ran through an unrecognizable heart. They settled in someone else's stomach and sat like stones. Her screams continued, rising higher and higher until Dr. Frankenstein used words like "hysterical" and "panic-stricken" and "for your own good." Her eyes were wide, the better to see you with, good doctor, as he raised his arm high, holding some sort of tool. He quickly brought it down on her head with a dull crack.

"Let's try this again," the voice said kindly. "For the second time, good morning, Marieke."

Second time is the charm. Second time is better than the first. A second set of eyes, a second wind, a second bite of the cherry.

Her eyelashes fluttered. They were butterflies. They were dusted with snow. They were running with tears.

"That's right. Welcome back. Again."

She focused on the doctor, who was wearing a white coat and that same sharp canine smile.

"Hmm?" she said. Her hands, unbound this time, beat at her throat. She caught sight of them, the fingers disjointed, sewn crudely to hands that didn't match each other. Her pinkie fingers both bent at the same odd angle.

"Hmm?"

Dr. Frankenstein took her hands gently in his. His fingers were long, the skin unbroken. His brown hands matched his brown wrists and brown arms. Envy. Want.

"My darling Marieke. There is so much to explain. But first, how are you? You seem much calmer this go around. This is good."

This is bad. This is wrong. Bad like the things she did to her daughters in the night. Bad like stealing from graves. Thoughts streamed through her head in different voices. Was one of them even hers?

She touched her throat again, her scarred and scabbed hands feeling around carefully.

"Yes, explore," the doctor encouraged. "You are a work of art. You are a wonder. If only you understood how truly special you are.

Her hands felt her shoulders.

The scapula, a voice said wistfully in her mind. It had a love for bones and human anatomy. It used to... what? Teach, maybe.

The skin there was rough, quite unlike her own originally.

"You're extraordinary," the doctor said. His eyes were brown and warm and blazed with a fire that was nearly feverish. "There's only been one other like you before. A man. But you are a woman. You are completely different."

Mandible, the voice breathed.

"There are so many differences between a man and a woman, aren't there? Look at your dainty hands, your slim legs. I found you the very best of legs. Won't you look down and see?"

Femur.

She peered down at her long, long legs. They stretched like unfurled ribbons, and she had that dizzy feeling of standing on a ladder that unexpectedly seemed too high.

"Oh, and your feet!" Frankenstein knelt in front of her abruptly, and she gasped deep in her throat

The hyoid bone.

but he was only being *excited,* this doctor, only showing her how her feet

Calcaneus. How exquisite!

were small and elegant and simply so pretty.

She caught a tiny flash of color on her instep.

Tarsals.

A piece of blue. She bent low, low, low, so far down to touch it, feeling that it was somehow something precious.

"Ah, yes. A tattoo. It looks like a forget-me-not. Of course, I'd rather you be unspotted, but that flower is the only unsightly thing. Look at your toes! The delicate arch of your foot! Yes, I, well, *we* personally went through dozens and dozens of feet to find the perfect pair, and here they are."

We? She asked her with eyes. Her mouth still didn't seem to be working. She straightened in horror when a white-haired man appeared behind the doctor.

"Allow me to introduce myself," he said. "I am Doctor Pretorius, and it is thanks to me that you were created at all."

I'm so tired, she thought, and the many parts of her agreed. Weary. Exhausted. She wanted to lie down and sleep forever. Again, whatever that meant. Yes, she wanted to sleep forever again.

The white-haired doctor continued talking but she wasn't listening. She touched her hair. It felt wild, certainly nothing like she had kept it in life.

Life? What...

"Here is your mate," the white-haired doctor announced, and swept his hand wide. "You were created for him."

Run, a voice said. It belonged to her legs. *I will run fast for you. I will carry us to safety.*

Fight, one hand whispered. *Hit and claw and snatch. I have long fingernails that will protect you.*

Scream, she thought, and it was her thought, her very own. *Scream and scare the monster away.*

Because it was a monster, tall and dark, wooden and pasted together like she was. His eyes were hooded, and his mouth was smiling, but everything about him seemed wrong. She looked at him, up and up and up, because he didn't stop until his head

cranium

nearly reached the sky.

"You are his bride," the white-haired doctor said, and the monster reached for her. His hands, the size of stone slabs. His arms, trunks of trees.

"I created him from pieces of the dead, just as I did you," Dr. Frankenstein said, his eyes fevered again. "Picked each piece and slid them together joint by joint. Aren't you two a wonder?"

She fell back, and her hands flew to her face.

Zygomatic bones, cooed the lover of bones.

"Friend?" the monster said and touched her dead hands with his dead hands.

I'm in pieces, the voices cried aloud, and there was horror, denial, torrential pain. *Pieces. Pieces of you. Pieces of me. Pieces of me making up YOU.*

"Bride?" the monster questioned. "Wife?"

"And children, eventually," White Hair said. "She has all the parts."

The monster held her shaking hand to his lips. Her stomach roiled. She tasted acid that had dried up long ago, back when the owner was killed. By a carriage or the fever or the plague. She didn't know, she didn't know. How had she died? Who was she? She was more than an incubator for this monster's seed. She had to be.

"Bride," the monster said again, and she screamed. She screamed, but it wasn't working. She couldn't open her mouth. She wrenched her hand from the monster's unwelcome kiss and touched her lips.

Wire. Puckered skin. Her lips had been sewn shut.

"We had to do it," Dr. Frankenstein said almost sheepishly. "Because of the earlier screaming, you know. It was just so loud and downright bothersome. But not to worry, because in time, when you've adjusted—"

She pushed past the doctors, past the monster, careening around on awkward legs that didn't quite work properly.

"Wife!" the monster cried and grabbed her wrist. She hissed at him like a swan through clenched teeth and buffeted him with her limbs. Her white, gauzy dress fell around her like wings, and she was a brilliant supernova, an angel in peril, and the monster grudgingly let her go.

"She hate me, like the others," he said, but she didn't care.

He's nothing to me, and her body urged her to go. Her hands grasped at the stone wall, and those fine feet carried her down slippery steps. She stumbled, her legs skidding out from under her, but she gathered herself and continued.

"Marieke!" the doctor screamed.

That wasn't her name.

"Bride!" the monster called.

That wasn't her name, either.

She didn't want to hear what White Hair would call her. She wouldn't conceive a child with that thing to satisfy some strange medical curiosity. It was cruel.

Cruel like my father. Like my brother. I'm the cruelest thing I know. Run. Flee.

She made it down the steps and crashed through dark, scrubby trees that surrounded the building. Tears ran down her face, seeping into the cracks and stitches that tacked her together.

Those that are dead ought to be left alone, she/her legs/her heart donor/someone thought, and the rest of them agreed. And that's what had happened, yes? She had died. She had been laid to rest. Marieke (*that's not my name*) was nothing more than a ghost trapped in a mobile body of cooled meat. She had been free and dragged back against her will. Her body was a house that she haunted.

Her lungs were full of decay and couldn't hold out any longer. She leaned against a tree, chest heaving, and tried to catch her breath. She was strangling. She was asphyxiating. She was going to die a second time, trapped in a body that wasn't hers. She scrabbled at her mouth but couldn't tear the wire away.

We're all going to die here, she thought. *I'm so very sorry.*

Maybe it's better this way, someone said inside of her. *We've all done this before. We're an abhorrence.*

Ah, but what's to stop them from making us again?

The woman not named Marieke froze, her breath caught tight in her lungs. The voice was right. They had made her before against her will. Wouldn't it be easier a second time?

She poised to flee again, but her legs were shaking.

I'm sorry, they said. *I seem to have run out of strength.*

Thank you, legs, she thought. *You've done so much.*

She patted her knee and ran her rough hand over her slim calf. Simply wonderful. She couldn't be prouder of their hard work.

Something clattered behind her, a person tripping over stone. Marieke (she'll just use this name as a placeholder for now, won't she?) dropped to her knees, holding her hands over her sutured mouth. She'd stay still like a baby bird, still like a statue, still like the corpse she once (all of them, really) had been.

"Marieke," called White Hair. She shuddered at his voice. Of all, he was by far the most frightening. "I know you haven't gone far. You're only thirty minutes old, after all. A newborn, really. Come back to us so we can take care of you."

Her right arm shook, wanting to swing an anvil. Wanting to shove its fingers down the doctor's throat until he choked on them.

Her left arm held the right gently, whispering that revenge could be had later, yes, but now was the time to be still, to be calm, to protect sweet Marieke and the others with stealth.

Marieke looked down to see her sore feet were torn and scratched nearly beyond recognition. The blue forget-me-not was covered in blood, and for that, she felt sorry.

Such a pretty little thing, she mused, but then her thoughts scattered.

There was a roaring, a chanting. It was a crowd, yelling at the top of their living, healthy lungs. People from the town, carrying wooden torches and sharp weapons that gleamed in the moonlight. Their cloaks looked damp from the earlier storm and they smelled like wet animals

Goats, a voice suggested helpfully. *Sheep. I cared for some in the village.*

and they swayed with an anger that was so looming, so enormous, that the force of it commanded Marieke to cower even lower.

The white-haired doctor cursed and crashed through the trees away from the mob. Marieke wanted to run, too, but she was stuck, her borrowed heart beating too hard for her unwieldy limbs.

"Monster," the people yelled. "Lunatic. Murderer."

"Fire," the monster cried, and its panicked voice yanked sympathy from Marieke. It was so frightened. How could something so big be that terrified?

Run, her body told her, and almost against her will, she stood. Her legs pushed and her arms pumped in unison. *Run, run, run.* She sprinted through trees and over gravel, not caring about the branches whipping her face and tangling into her matted hair. She had to escape. She had already fled monsters, and now she was fleeing monster killers. After all, she thought idly, she was a monster herself.

Sleep. Drink. She found a steam and put her battered mouth to it, the water sliding in between the sutures. It tasted fresh. It tasted familiar. How many times had she, had *they,* partaken from this same stream in their lives?

Many. Several. Never. They all had different answers.

She was covered in sweat and dirt. Blood smeared her arms and legs, caking into the rough spots and infecting her stitches. She was a rag doll held together by refuse and twine. She slipped off her white dress and stepped into the water to wash.

Carefully, carefully, she scrubbed her
Clavicle.
and her *humerus,* and her *radius.*

She unearthed her new body, beautiful and strong, able to stand and run and tell her stories about itself.

I used to be a dancer, I think. Yes, I used to dance.

The first time I killed a man, my heart soared. I thought I would feel guilt, but I did not.

I can teach you to make flower chains if you'd like. We can make a crown of forget-me-nots.

She ended at her feet, patting them tenderly and pulling them from the water. She stood on the rocks to dry.

"Oh," said a voice from behind her. Marieke spun around.

"Oh," the voice said again. It belonged to a young woman with braids. Her brown eyes opened wider until the whites showed all around.

Marieke primed herself to run, but her body was weary. Her knees knocked together awkwardly, and it was almost like they hadn't belonged to a dancer at all. She fell, landing on the rocks with a muffled cry.

"Oh," the woman said a third time, and she held her hands out. Soft hands. Perfect hands. They matched the skin of her face beautifully. Uncut and untorn.

"Are you all right?" The girl asked. She took a step forward but paused when Marieke jolted. "I don't mean to scare you. I'm actually quite frightened myself."

The girl squatted and wrapped her arms around her knees. She took deep breaths, in and out.

This is so she won't be as afraid, a voice told her. *She always did that.*

Marieke started. *Do you know her?* she thought.

No. Never seen her before. Yes, perhaps. She may have came to the shop once, the voices said.

I think we have the same eyes.

That last thought, wispy and almost uninterested, brought Marieke up short. She looked at the girl in a new light. She blinked. She looked at her with first one eye, and then the other. Even with both eyes, the girl looked like a stranger.

"Are you cold?" the girl asked. "Would you like your dress?"

Marieke stared at her, but the girl didn't move. Yes, she wanted her dress. No, she didn't want that filthy thing anywhere near her. She waited for the young woman to decide, to make the decision for her, but the girl simply waited.

Marieke nodded sharply. The girl stood up, picked up the billowing dress, and hesitated.

"I'm going to bring it to you," she said. "I'll come slowly, and I won't get too close. Is that all right?"

Again, Marieke and her body waited, but the girl stood still.

"I won't come without your permission," the girl said.

Permission. Marieke growled deep in her throat. The girl went white, and her fingers clutched the dress more tightly.

Marieke closed her eyes. She tried to school her face into something less repulsive, less monstrous. She nodded and gestured clumsily for the girl to come.

"Here," said the girl, and her lips opened so very wide and perfectly, as she spoke. Marieke pulled the dress over her head, looking away as the girl studied her scars openly.

"Does it hurt?" the girl asked.

Marieke shook her head.

"Did you have an accident?"

Another head shake. Not an accident, per se, but rather an affront to God.

"My sister," the girl said, and her voice did a funny thing, a sad thing. She coughed and tried again. "My sister met a man who had wounds like yours. She was just a little girl. Her name was Maria. Did you know my sister Maria?"

No, she didn't.

"Maria liked to play. They said she was playing with a monster. They said he drowned her and ran away. This monster had stitches just like yours. The villagers are out trying to find him."

Marieke bent over and wept. She covered her face with her strange hands.

Maria, a voice murmured. *That might have been my name.*

"Don't cry," the girl said, and reached out with an unsteady hand. "It isn't your fault. I just wanted to—"

She stopped suddenly, staring at the Marieke's hands. At her little fingers, the way they were so much smaller than the rest of them, the way they bent at odd angles.

When the girl spoke, her voice was very calm.

"Are you alive, miss?"

Still weeping, Marieke nodded.

"Were you made from the dead?"

A wail, muted from the twine. A scream, torn from a throat that belonged to someone else. Agony that belonged to all of them.

"May I touch your hands?"

Marieke held one hand to her broken face and extended the other toward the girl. They trembled. They shivered. They remembered touch, what it felt like to be held by another, and that feeling was

sensational

horrible

comforting.

Are you going to break me? a voice thought. *Can I bloody my fist against your face? Hold my hand and keep me safe. Rip my fingers from this beastly body.*

Sister.

Sister. That voice was the loudest, a sigh, and a flurry of satisfaction bubbled up from far below. Sister.

The girl touched Marieke's hands gingerly, then ran her fingers over her crooked pinkie. She bent her head and kissed it, clasping it to her breast.

"Oh, it's you. It's you, Maria. I'd recognize these darling little fingers anywhere."

Marieke shrank back. This was where the girl would rage at her, would spill her fury from her flawless rosebud mouth with its working tongue. This was where she would grab a weapon (*my knife, my scissors, my axe*) and dismember Marieke's hands. She'd steal her ill-gotten fingers and secret her darling little Maria away in a drawer somewhere.

She was ready. Marieke squeezed her eyes closed and stilled herself.

When the girl moved, she moved quickly, like a garden snake. She reached down and touched the forget-me-not on Marieke's instep.

"This. I know this mark. This was my friend Sanne. She was a shepherdess. Oh, she was so dear to me!"

Marieke was a tree nailed together with loved ones. She was a fiend made up of children and abusers. She wanted to say that she was sorry. She wanted to wrest her own joints and throw these precious parts to the girl, who would treasure them more than she ever could. She caught the girl's hand, staring her directly in the eyes.

"Oh no," the girl whispered. "They're coming."

Marieke didn't understand. Who was coming? The

ghosts? They were already here. They dwelled inside her. She didn't know how to let them go.

"The villagers," the girl said, and her eyes went wild. "They're chasing the monster. They mustn't find you. Come with me."

She grabbed Marieke by the hand, (*so good, so warm, so uncomfortable, pssh*) and pulled her to her feet. Marieke stumbled over the hem of her dress, but the girl righted her. The girl's arm was wiry and strong, her steps nimble, and Marieke ran with her.

"Monster! Monster!" the villagers cried. Their voices were a sea, and their torches were an inferno. Marieke looked up to see the doctor's laboratory on the hill was ablaze.

"Don't look, just run," the girl called, and Marieke obeyed. She pulled her body together and they worked as one, concentrating to move in sync.

The shepherdess kicked up her heels to avoid rocks. Maria found the fastest way through the brush. The blacksmith took the hardy blows of the branches they could not dodge. To safety, to safety. Nobody would disassemble this little Maria again without Marieke's say-so.

"To the old shed," the girl cried, and they burst out of the trees and into grasses. They flew, they flew, hand-in-hand, sisters together, and Maria trilled deep inside Marieke's head.

I never thought I would hold my sister's hand again.

The shed was built of stone. They crashed inside and the girl quickly pulled the door behind them. They huddled together in the dark, their arms (and arms and arms and arms) around each other, holding tight.

"I can't lose you again, Maria," the girl said, and kissed her sister's fingers desperately.

"And you," she said, patting Marieke's tumbled mane in the dark, "I can't lose you, either. You're made up out of all that is special, and you are special yourself."

Marieke's heart burned like the mob's torches. She tried to say thank you, but her bloody lips held fast.

"Shh," the girl said in a low voice. "They're still coming."

"Kill the monster. Kill the doctors," the crowd chanted. They grew closer. Their footsteps sounded like an army in metal armor, not peasants in soft leather. "Kill kill kill!"

"We saw you run in there, lass," a man bellowed. "Saw the way you move. You aren't natural."

The heavy door flew open, and the girl squealed. Marieke blinked at the blinding torch light obscuring the faces of her executioners.

"Girl, quick. We're here to save you." A woman reached forward and grabbed the girl by the arm, but she struggled.

"No! No, she isn't hurting me. She is not one of them."

The crowd surged. It was made up of a million voices just like Marieke was. It moved to and fro like an insect, with limbs upon limbs upon limbs darned together with fury and hate, just as Marieke was strung with twine and bruised skin.

"She's under its influence. The monster must be burned!"

A man with red hair grabbed the girl by her ankles and yanked. She slid across the rocky ground, away from Marieke and toward the crowd. As soon as she was out of reach, men advanced with pitchforks and field scythes. Marieke cowered.

"No, look," the girl cried. "She is kind. She didn't do this to herself. Who sews their own mouth shut? Who creates their own body from parts of the dead?"

"The dead?"

"Blasphemy."

"Repulsive."

"Monster!"

"She is made up of Maria," the girl shouted, clambering to her feet. She stood straight and tall, her braids blowing in the wind. Marieke had never seen a more powerful sight in her life. "Do you see? Look at her fingers, Ma," she cried, looking around the crowd. "Ma, I know you're here! Come and see."

The villagers undulated, arguing loudly until a woman pushed her way to the front.

"Ma," the girl said gently. "Don't be frightened. She won't hurt you." She turned toward Marieke. "May I see your hands, please?"

Marieke held them out, palms up. They quivered, her bare wrists exposed to the blades of the townspeople's daggers and scythes. Who knew such a simple act could be so vulnerable?

The girl reached out and clasped her hands. Then she turned them over.

"Ma, touch them. It's Maria."

Her mother

I love my mother. I hate my mother. I never had a mother.

touched the odd little fingers gently, first one, and then the other.

Mama.

"It's her," she said, and fell to the ground. Marieke fell with her, touching her face with her daughter's fingers.

"Stay back," the man with red hair said. He lunged forward, but the girl grabbed his wrist.

"Idiot, your sister is here, too. Do you see?"

She pointed at the blue tattoo on Marieke's foot. The man gawked.

"Could it really be?"

He bent and touched the mark with a sure hand. He stared hard into Marieke's eyes.

"You didn't choose this? This was done to you?"

She nodded and wiggled her toes gently. She wanted to say, "Your sister lives on in me," but naturally she couldn't get the words out.

The man's eyes were hooded.

"Is she in pain?"

Marieke shook her head.

"Do you...can you feel her?" he asked hoarsely.

She nodded, and touched her heart, and then her head. *Here. And here.*

"Is she happy?"

She smiled as much as she could, wishing she could speak, and then—

"Ah, you have found her," Dr. Frankenstein said. "I'm so very relieved. Now if you would excuse me, I'd like to take her home now."

The doctor's face looked grotesque in the glow of the torches, moving unnaturally in the shadows.

The red-haired man stood, his eyes blazing with firelight and fury.

"What gives you the right?" he asked.

Dr. Frankenstein bowed his head politely. "I have every right. I created her. Right up in that laboratory that you fellows so gleefully demolished, if I do say. She hasn't caused any trouble has she, my dear little Marieke?"

"Marieke?"

The people in the crowd tasted her name. It rolled around on their tongues like gristle, like fat, like pieces of leaves they chewed when they could not find anything else.

"It means 'beloved,'" the doctor said. "And she is so very beloved. She was created to rival the gods."

"And to be a mate," the white-haired doctor said. Marieke hadn't heard him approach. "She was born to be a bride."

"Marieke also means 'bitter,'" a woman holding a dagger said. "From the looks of her, she wants nothing to do with you two gentlemen." The last word was a sneer, and the crowd pressed close behind her. "I think perhaps you two should be on your way."

"We'll go," White-Hair said, and held his grasping claw out to Marieke, "as soon as she comes with us. She doesn't belong to you."

"Doesn't belong—?" The woman scoffed. "Surely you speak in jest. She belongs to nobody but herself. Her body, though? Those parts were stolen."

The girl stood between White-Hair and Marieke.

"Her fingers belonged to my sister Maria."

The man with red hair joined her.

"I recognize my sister's foot. It's marked in blue, and impossible to mistake."

"I think those are my daughter's legs," a man piped up. "She adored dancing."

One by one, the people of the mob stood, crowding between Marieke and the doctors. Marieke slowly got to her feet, staring at the farm tools that were being used for her, and not against her.

Did you ever in your life? a voice whispered. She could feel the awe coming from it.

No. No, never did she ever, not in her short life.

Her stolen heart soared. It pumped her blood so quickly that her cheeks colored in wonder. Her hand stole to the side of her face.

"We'll protect you," the girl said, and took her hand easily. "There are many of us and only two of them. You aren't in danger anymore."

But a doctor doesn't become a doctor by simply being brilliant. He becomes one by being driven, and persistent, and ever-so-slightly mad.

"Come, come," Dr. Frankenstein said, and clapped his hands. The villagers went quieted. He pushed his hair out of his face and smiled tightly.

"I'm certain we can work something out," he said. "What would you like for her? Perhaps a little trade? A young wife and mother who died suddenly, perhaps? Wouldn't it be wonderful if she were reanimated to raise her brood? Or perhaps a strong man who protected the village? We could do some enhancements so he can swing an axe three times as long as he could before without wearying. Hmm?"

Marieke chilled. Her blood stopped. Her joints moaned and her stitches ached. They were going to turn her over. She was going to be trapped by these feral doctors and bedded by the monster. After all, as White-Hair said, she had all the parts.

The woman with the dagger eyed the doctors, and then walked to Marieke. The crowd parted for her.

She took the knife, turning it in the firelight so it shone, and then glared at Marieke. Marieke stood unblinking.

The woman whirled, holding the dagger high.

"You've said enough. Prattle, prattle, that's all that's come from your mouths. I'm tired of it."

She pressed the dagger into Marieke's mismatched hands. The hilt was warm, and the blade was sharp.

"Do as you will," the woman said. "The choice is yours."

Marieke held the dagger to her cheek and closed her eyes. She could leap at White-Hair and gash his throat. She could stop her own heart. She could rip apart her limbs and give everything back.

She opened her eyes and looked at the girl. The girl's lips turned up quickly and then fell away, the tiniest hint of a smile.

She always did that, Marie murmured.

Marieke pressed the blade to her skin, testing its sharpness. Then she used it to slash at the wires suturing her mouth shut. Blood ran from her lips, but she didn't stop until she had worked her way through. The wire fell in pieces to the ground.

She opened her mouth to speak.

THE INVISIBLE MAN

JEFF DEPEW

Human beings are social animals. As a species, we prefer—no, we *need*—to live alongside other people. Complete isolation causes psychological problems. We disassociate from others, and in doing so, we disassociate from ourselves. I have always believed that. When this story began, I hadn't had an actual face-to-face conversation with another human being in almost two years, and it was starting to wear on me.

Let me start at the beginning. My name is Jack Griffin. I was born and raised in a small town in Indiana. I won't bother telling you the name- you've never heard of it. Anyway, after high school, I had two options: work for my dad and older brother painting houses, or... No, forget that. That was my only option. So, instead, I joined the Army. Have you ever painted a house? It's not as much fun as it looks. My family was pissed, especially my father, but it didn't really matter. I cut contact with them, in '66, right after I joined the army. Just in time for a trip to Vietnam.

I liked the Army. They tell you when to get up, when to eat, when to shit. And I had a knack for it. I did well in reconnaissance. Me and my unit would go in and see what we could see. Sometimes we'd act, sometimes we'd let the grunts handle it. Observe and report. Those were our orders. Most of the time. But I got my hands dirty a few times.

I was pretty good at recon. Now and then, when I lay awake at three in the morning, thinking about it, I realized I was probably *too* good. I did some things that I'm not proud of. Things I'll never forget, no matter how badly I want to.

In 1978 I was asked to volunteer for an important study. I was bored, to be honest. I missed the action.

They called it the Human Cloaking Program." HCP. "This could change the future of reconnaissance and espionage," they told me. "You'll be doing a great service for your country," they said. "Gotta beat the Commies," I was told. "You'll be a human bullet," some major had said. Whatever that means.

Of course, I had agreed. Couldn't let the Russians have the first invisible comrade. And really, what else did I have to do? There was nothing for me back in the States. By that time, my mom had been dead for a few years and Dad was in a home. My brother sent me a Christmas card every year. Got to hand it to him, he never gave up on me.

As soon as I signed my name, I was whisked away to a military hospital at Fort Bliss in El Paso, Texas, where doctors poked and prodded and tested me for two weeks straight. *This isn't so bad*, I remember thinking. It hurt sometimes, but pain is temporary. Some other guys were going through the same program as me. I'd see them here and there, getting their shots, being wheeled into rooms. But we were never allowed to interact. I slept, showered, and ate by myself.

After weeks of all those tests and shots... nothing. I spent two months with my thumb up my ass, watching TV, exploring the base, and basically waiting. Nothing. I got to know El Paso pretty well. I must have walked around every inch of that city they had, hit every bar in town.

I figured that was it. They'd forgotten about me, I'd failed the test, whatever.

But I was wrong. One night two MP's and a guy in a white suit showed up at my favorite bar at two in the morning, pulled me outside, shoved me in the back of a civilian car, and drove me to the airfield. I was blindfolded and put on a plane. After a two or three-hour flight, they drove me, still blindfolded, to another military base. Only this one wasn't on any maps. I know. I've looked.

Long story short, I spent six months or so—it's hard to tell—in an underground lab, somewhere *not* in El Paso, where I was poked and prodded all over again. Only this time, I was also given injections and pills and was even operated on at least twice (that I know of). I would show you the scars, but you wouldn't be able to see them.

They messed with my adrenal gland. That's all I know; I'm no scientist. I overheard some doctors talking. And I'm pretty sure once when they had me opened up, they put something in me. In my head. Some kind of electronic tracker so they could keep tabs on me. I've tried to find it, but it's in there deep.

So here it is: they made me invisible. I'm the Invisible Man. It took a while to get used to. Have you ever run downstairs without looking at your feet? Climbing down a ladder without seeing your hands? And shaving? Forget the razor blade. I use an electric shaver. It's surprising how not being able to see your hands and feet makes things harder.

Anyway, after some more training, they flew me to

Eastern Europe, and I was back in it. I continued my work in reconnaissance, only this time, they didn't send in anyone else. They would drop me off alone, I'd acquire the target, eliminate the target, then head home. It wasn't bad. It's a little hard to remember all of it. I think because of that thing they put in my head. Or maybe because I don't want to remember.

Just before we decided to get out of Afghanistan, the Army shut down HCP. It was too expensive and apparently, I was their only success. Yet the question remained: *What do we do with our real-life invisible man?* Turning me back to the way I was before was out of the question.

So they retired me. Full pension. Just like that. No "thank you", no medal, just, "Don't let the door hit you in the ass on the way out." But I knew they wouldn't get rid of me. I was their insurance policy in case the Russians *did* create their own invisible man.

I moved up here a few years ago. I have a handler, Major Wells, who calls and checks up on me every couple of weeks. "How are you feeling?" "Do you need anything?" Stuff like that. There's an Army base a few hours away and they send a truckload of groceries up every six months. Mostly canned stuff and K-rations. Like I didn't have enough of those when I was serving. Sometimes they send booze.

But here I am, five years later, living in a small two-bedroom house in Hillmon, Michigan, where it's cold as hell and snows for six months out of the year if we're lucky. It's way up in the Upper Peninsula area of Michigan. Even though the town is small, it's pretty spread out, so I have my privacy. And the cold weather makes it easier for me to go out all bundled up so I don't look conspicuous. I like it well enough. Folks here are very friendly and mind their own business.

The army did give me some latex prosthetics: a fake nose and ears, and even some realistic flesh-colored makeup, but I really only used them when I was busting to get outside. The prosthetics were fine as long as someone didn't get a good look. You stayed too long in one place and people stared. They knew something was up. Accident victim? Burn victim with bad plastic surgery? Too much staring. It made me uncomfortable. Even before I "lost" my body, I never liked being the center of attention. I don't understand people at sporting events and game shows who get all excited that they're on TV and jump up and down like idiots. Like somehow it validates who they are.

I've always preferred to sit on the sidelines. In the winter, I went out. I had a '68 Ford Bronco and a snowmobile. I kept them under the covered carport. I'd use the garage, but it's full of junk from the previous owner and it smells nasty like something died in there. Probably a raccoon. I've heard them up in the attic.

When it was too warm and wearing a ski mask would draw attention, I stayed home. I kept my pantry stocked so I could lay low. I read a lot. I fished in the pond out behind my house. I took long walks at night.

I exercised when I could. Just because I couldn't see my body didn't mean I wanted to get fat. I spent late evenings jogging, doing pull-ups and sit-ups and pushups. A white undershirt, track pants, and basketball shoes. And If I was feeling really hip, maybe a bandana.

I also watched a lot of TV. And read. Thank God for the Book of the Month Club. But I was bored. Bored and lonely. At least when I was serving, I could have conversations. But not now. Just quick interactions at the market or a drive-through restaurant.

Winter was here. There was about two feet of snow on

the ground, and while I was making coffee one morning, I heard a couple of rifle blasts. Deer season had started. I went hunting a couple of times when I first got here. Bundled all up, goggles and face mask, with my camo gear and orange vest, I looked like all the other goofballs. But I haven't been hunting in a while. It brought back a lot of bad memories.

I opened the freezer and scanned the frozen dinners. Only a couple left. I was running low. During dinner—Salisbury steak, accompanied by mashed potatoes, corn, and a glass of whiskey, if you're wondering—I decided to go on a shopping trip. Besides, I was getting a little antsy. I hadn't been out of the house in a couple of days, and besides the frozen dinners, I was getting low on other stuff too. Wells had not sent a shipment in a while. I'd call him, but he never gave me his number.

Eating for me wasn't like in the movies. In the movies, when an invisible man eats, you can see the food as it's chewed and then swallowed. But not me. When I put something in my mouth, you couldn't see it. When I was first turned invisible, I ate in front of a mirror. As soon as I put the food in my mouth, it was gone. I could hold small objects in my hand and they couldn't be seen until I opened it. Small folding knives, a loop of piano wire. Things like that.

I watched TV until about two in the morning, but I wasn't really watching. There was never anything good on. I decided I would pick up some new VHS tapes. I dressed in my cold-weather gear and boots. No socks. No underwear. Easy on and easy off. I drove to town, about twenty minutes away down a dark, winding road. I didn't see anyone else, which was always a good sign for my "shopping" trips.

I rolled onto Main Street and cruised around for a bit.

Everything was shut up. No stragglers or drunks walking around. I made a left and headed for the Sav-More. There were a couple of cars in the parking lot, but no people around. Maybe the cars had dead batteries, the owners got rides. I drove around the back and pulled in by the rear loading dock. There was a security camera at the far end of the parking lot, but I avoided it. I'd done this before.

It wasn't too hard to make my way into the store. There was a window about eight feet high. I just pushed a dumpster under it, and I could easily reach it and climb in. It was never locked. I took off my clothes and folded them on the driver's seat. It was freezing, so I hurried. I scrambled onto the dumpster and pushed the window open and slithered into an office.

The only thing I wore was a pair of black socks. Those tile floors are cold in the middle of the night.

The window emptied out into a loft filled with boxes, an old cash register, and some ancient display signs. I went down the stairs into the storeroom. There was an alarm box mounted on the wall beside the loading door, but no lights were on. I don't even think it worked. There were no cameras in the store. Not that that would matter to me. They'd see a cart moving around by itself, although that probably would raise suspicion. So "no cameras here" was good.

I moved out to the front of the store and grabbed a shopping cart. I went aisle to aisle, taking what I needed. Frozen meat, some TV dinners, cereal, soup, some VHS tapes, two cases of beer, and a few bottles of whiskey and vodka. I wandered into the produce section and grabbed a bag of potatoes, some oranges, and some apples. America is an amazing country. Oranges in December. In Michigan.

Something brushed against my leg. I looked down at a

fluffy orange cat winding between my bare legs. The store cat. I'd seen him before. I think his name was Milo or something. I nudged him away and kept moving.

I rolled through the clothing aisles and stocked up on underwear and some jeans. Then I swung through the sporting goods section. I wanted a new gun. I didn't like hunting, but I could always go shooting.

I couldn't find the keys anywhere, so I had to force open the gun cabinet, but I got a nice Dakota hunting rifle and a few boxes of ammo. I closed the case as best I could, but it was still broken. Maybe they wouldn't notice.

When the cart was full, and I was really getting cold, I headed to the rear loading dock. I propped the rear door open, loaded up my truck, pushed the cart back inside, and put the cart back where I found it. I went up the stairs and pulled the window closed. Before I closed the back door, I checked to make sure Milo hadn't gotten out.

Fifteen minutes later I was in my carport unloading my groceries. Five minutes after that, I was frying up a big steak and drinking some bourbon. That's the last thing I remember until the ringing phone woke me from a deep, drunken sleep. I sat up and blinked beneath the bright-white kitchen light.

I was sitting at the kitchen table. The side of my head hurt. The remains of a steak sat on a plate in front of me, and a half-full whiskey bottle stood beside my chair. My head was thick like it was full of oatmeal and broken glass. It took me a few seconds to get my bearings. The phone rang again. I reached out a hand and clawed the old plastic phone off the wall hook.

"Hello," I muttered.

"Griffin," said a rough, business-like voice. Wells. What did he want so late?

"Yeah...who else would it be?" I said.

"I know it's late, but I thought you should know. Are you alone?"

I barked a humorless laugh. "I'm always alone. Thanks to you and the Army."

"Never mind that," he said. "There's... a situation."

I sobered up a little. "Yeah. What kind of situation?"

"The CIA has completely closed the books on the Human Cloaking Program."

"I know," I said. "They did that years ago." I cradled the phone between my chin and shoulder and filled my coffee urn with water. I needed to wake up. Fast.

"Well, they did, but they didn't. They just kept it quiet. But now they've *officially* shut it down. They're focusing on invisible materials now - fabric, and metal plates for tanks, things like that."

"Okay," I said, turning on the coffee maker. I slid back into my chair. "So, what does this mean for me?" But a small inkling of an idea was forming. A not so good idea.

"You're the last loose end, Griffin. Everything else has been torched." He paused. I heard the clink of glass on glass. *Was he drinking?* "They're coming for you."

I reached for my own bottle and took a swallow. I wiped my mouth with the back of my hand. When I spoke, my voice was raw. "When?"

"Soon," Wells said. "They landed in-state at 0300."

I glanced up at the yellow sunflower clock above the stove. It was nearly six. If they landed at three, they could be here within the hour. I looked out the kitchen window. Still dark out.

"Okay," I said. There wasn't much more to say.

Wells cleared his throat. "This conversation never

happened. I'm calling from off-base. But... I just thought you should know. "

"Okay, "I said again. "Thanks."

"I don't know what you're talking about," Wells said and hung up.

I never heard from him again.

I moved from room to room, making sure the windows were locked and pulling the shades down. The sun wouldn't be up for a couple more hours. I went into the spare bedroom where I kept all my service weapons and gear. I stripped down and pulled on a military snowsuit. There's more than one way to be invisible. I grabbed a handgun—a Ruger P90—and some extra magazines, which I stuck in various pockets. I went to the living room, picked up my new rifle, sat on the couch, and loaded it.

I stood at the front window, pulled back the curtains, and looked around. It was still dark. They could be outside right now, watching the house. Whoever "they" was. CIA? Special Forces? It could be two of them or ten. I had to be ready.

I moved to the back of the house, through the kitchen, keeping low, and let myself out the back door. The only road to my house was out front. I wanted to be behind them when they showed up. I moved through my backyard, the snow crunching beneath my boots, pushing my way through the underbrush until I found an opening. There was an old deer trail, a rough path through the trees. I had a clear view of the rear of the house and would be able to see if anyone came around on either side. I squatted down and waited.

Time passed. A bird landed on a nearby branch and looked toward me, its beady eyes unreadable, chirped once, then flitted away. Other than that, I was alone.

Morning came slowly. The trees gradually detached themselves from the darkness. I squirmed restlessly. I debated stripping down now, but as long as I had the guns, it didn't matter. I would be invisible, but the guns wouldn't. And I needed the pockets for ammo.

After about half an hour, I heard a soft voice. Someone was coming. I knelt down, making myself as small as possible, and waited. I clicked the safety off the rifle and swung the barrel toward the approaching voices.

I heard the sound of feet, at least two pairs, maybe three. I leaned forward to get a better look. There they were. Three of them. I could just make them out through the branches. They were wearing full camouflage gear and carrying rifles. I slowly stretched out my legs until I was laying flat on the ground and aimed.

One of them, the tallest one, was doing all the talking, pointing, and giving instructions to the other two. I'd take him out first. I lowered my head and sighted down the barrel. The guy was scolding one of the other two. I fired, and a crimson blossom appeared in the center of his chest. He stumbled back as the other two looked around. I fired again and caught him in the throat. I could hear his thin, reedy scream in the crisp air. He toppled onto his back. One of the others crouched beside him and I shot him in the back. He fell beside his leader.

The third figure spun and ran. I fired again but missed. Bark exploded from a tree just above him. He sprinted out of sight.

"Shit," I said, and stood up, dropping my rifle. I pulled the zipper down and stepped out of my winter camo snowsuit and picked up the Ruger handgun. I kicked off the boots and ran after the fleeing figure. I wasn't sure if he was the only one left, but either way I couldn't let him go. I ran, keeping the gun low, making it harder to be seen. He was following the deer trail, so there was little room to maneuver. Still, I was getting scratched to shit.

I sprinted past the two bodies, not even glancing down. I'd deal with them later. I couldn't feel the cold; I was too ramped up by the chase. I hadn't felt like this in years: this combination of fear and excitement. I guess I missed the action. I slowed and listened. It was dead quiet.

But there! A twig snapped. I whirled toward the sound, raising the gun, but didn't see anything. I moved toward the sound, staying low, staying quiet. A flash of green behind a tree. He stepped out from behind the tree and swept his rifle barrel up toward me.

I ran at him, extending the gun at him. His eyes widened and he stepped back, not sure what he was seeing. A floating gun? I fired one, twice, three times, and he fell back against the tree.

I stood over him, breathing hard. One of his eyes was gone, replaced with a raw black hole leaking blood onto his cheek. He was young. Really young. Or maybe I was just getting old. I grabbed his legs and pulled him away from the tree and rolled him into a ditch. If more were coming, they'd find him eventually. If not, the wolves would.

I headed back. I checked on the other two I'd shot. The first one, the leader, was dead. The other one was still alive. Short, quick breaths. I'd hit him in the back. Probably punctured his lung. I pushed my bare foot on the back of his head and shoved his face deep into the snow. He jerked weakly, and his legs kicked once or twice, so I pushed harder, putting my weight into it. His breathing slowed, then stopped. I counted to one hundred before I stepped off him. He wasn't moving anymore. I put my foot back on his head and counted to one hundred again. I was careful. I knelt and searched them for radios. Nothing. Just more ammunition and a set of keys. I took the keys. I'd have to find their car and move it.

I pulled the two corpses off the trail and covered them with branches as best I could. All the while, I kept an eye out for more of them. There had to be more.

I hurried back to where I'd left my snowsuit and put it on. Oh, sweet relief. Let me tell you, invisibility has its benefits but warm is warm. I made a wide circle around my house and then camped across the street. I lay down beneath a big pine tree. I could see the front of my house. I was careful. I've always been careful.

The sun struggled through the overcast sky all morning. Eventually, when I judged it to be around noon, I stood up. My back was stiff from the cold, and I stretched, twisting from side to side, looking around for anything unusual. Satisfied, I hurried across the road from my house. I lit a fire in the living room and I placed the car keys and my Ruger on the coffee table in front of the couch. I stripped off the snowsuit and stretched again, warming myself in front of the fire.

When I was warm enough, I went into the kitchen and poured a cup of coffee. Then I moved my armchair so it was facing the front door. I picked up the Ruger and waited.

Something woke me. A noise. I sat up and grabbed my Ruger. Moved to the front window. I heard the crunch of tires on snow. I pulled the curtain aside just a tiny bit and peeked out. Two police cars idled in the driveway. What could they want? Maybe Wells had sent them as protection?

But that didn't make sense. Nobody was supposed to know I was here.

There was a knock at the door. I didn't make a sound. Maybe they'd leave if they didn't think I was home. Footsteps moved around the side of the house, and I heard muffled voices. Another knock at the door.

The kitchen door knob rattled behind me. Somebody was trying to get in.

What if they weren't cops? The front door knob turned. Had I forgotten to lock it? I slid behind an armchair and lowered the gun so it couldn't be seen. If I needed to use it, they wouldn't see it until it was too late.

The front door opened slightly. Nobody came in. "Hello? Anybody home?" A voice called. "This is Sheriff Perryman. We'd like to ask you a few questions."

The door opened wider and the sheriff, a short, stocky man entered, followed by a deputy. Their hands were empty.

"Anybody home?" the sheriff said, stepping into the living room. "We need to ask you a few-" He looked right past me and he froze. He reached out and grabbed the deputy by the arm, who glanced over.

They stared at me. Not *at* me, obviously, but through me. I'm not sure what they were looking at. The gun felt hot in my hands, and I was tempted to pull it out and use it. But I'd wait. I'd stand perfectly still, and they'd look around, not find anything, and leave.

A third deputy came in behind the other two. He saw where they were looking and stared.

"Sir," said the sheriff. He had a hand on his holster. He was still looking in my direction. "Are you Mr. Wells? Is it okay if we come in? We're trying to find some missing hunters."

Wells? Wells was thousands of miles from here. How would he even know about Wells? Were they even cops?

The sheriff turned and whispered something to the deputy on his left, who nodded and moved down the hallway into the kitchen. The sheriff and the first deputy stepped into the living room. The deputy moved over by the window. The sheriff kept his hand on the butt of his revolver.

"Sir," he said again, but with more command. "Mr. Wells? Are you home? We tried to call but your phone was disconnected."

I didn't budge, didn't breathe. Why were they looking at me? A movement out of the corner of my eye. I turned my head. The second deputy coming from the kitchen was moving behind me.

"He's got a gun!" he shouted and ducked back into the kitchen.

Fuck it. That was it. I raised the gun and fired at the sheriff. Then I spun toward the deputy. I heard more shots. Something punched me in the shoulder and I spun and fell back onto the floor. Something was wrong, I remembered thinking. Then everything went black.

I woke up here in a hospital bed I think two... maybe three days ago. It's hard to tell. I'm pretty drugged up. I had a tube in my nose when I first woke up, but it's gone now. My left shoulder was all wrapped up and my arm was in a sling. The first time I tried to sit up, I realized my right arm was cuffed to the railing that ran alongside the bed. I slept a lot. I had vague recollections of people coming and going. Nurses, doctors, cops.

I felt more alert when I woke up this morning. Maybe they cut back on the drugs.

But none of this made sense. How could I have been shot? Why was I cuffed to the bed? I looked around the room. Several machines sat alongside one wall, humming softly. Beside my bed was a metal bedside table. The only thing on it was a water cup.

I hated hospitals. I had spent too much time in one when they experimented on me. I had to get out of here. But I'd be patient. Lay low, nice, and quiet. Maybe they'd forget about me if they couldn't see me. I was used to waiting.

On the far side of the room across from my bed, the door was partially open. Beside it was a window that looked out into the corridor. A cop sat against the window, his back to me, leaning his hid against the glass. He looked like he might be sleeping. He suddenly stiffened and stood up. Four figures came into view and stood beside him: two more cops and a guy in a suit. And someone in a military uniform.

"So, what are we looking at?" I recognized the sheriff's gruff voice.

The guy in the suit, probably a detective, turned. "We positively identified the bodies as the missing hunters." A pause. "Phillip Mathers, 42, and his sons: Michael, 15, and Thomas, 10."

"Jesus," one of the cops said.

"And what about the body in the garage?"

"Well, that one is so decomposed that we can't ID it yet. We're having an M.E. come up from Traverse City tomorrow. But all indications are that it's Graham Wells, the owner of the house. Nobody's seen him for months, so it's possible."

None of this made sense. That was my house. There was no dead body in the garage. I went in there... actually, I couldn't remember the last time I'd been in the garage.

And what about the three assassins sent after me? Didn't they find those bodies?

"And what do we know about this guy?" said the sheriff.

"I can handle that," said the guy in the Army uniform. "This guy's a fucking nightmare. He's former army. He escaped from a psych ward in Arizona about two years ago, after stabbing his doctor and two orderlies and went AWOL. He's been on the run ever since. Diagnosed schizophrenic."

Who were they talking about?

"And he's been living here for how long?"

The detective stepped forward. "Based on Wells' body, about a year."

The sheriff stepped forward. "Before we went by, we tried to call the house, but the phone's been out for about six months. No wi-fi, no cable. Just gas and electricity. Apparently, Wells had those on autopay through his bank, and after he died, they kept paying."

This didn't make any sense. I spoke to Wells on the phone just the other night. And I watched TV every night. Just the other day I watched... I couldn't remember.

One of the cops leaned into the doorway and looked in my room.

"He's awake," he said.

The detective and the Army guy, a major—I saw his oak leaf—stepped into the doorway and looked at my bed.

"As soon as he's well enough to travel, we'll be taking him." He spun on his heel and left.

"Now wait just a god damned minute," said the sheriff, hurrying after him, followed by the two uniforms. "He killed four people in my town. He's not going anywhere."

The detective stayed behind, staring at me.

"You're in quite a bit of trouble, my friend. It seems like

everyone wants a piece of you," he said. "You have anything to say for yourself?"

I stayed quiet and I didn't move. He couldn't see me. No one can see me. Eventually I'll escape. I'm patient. And once I do, they'll never find me. I'm the invisible man.

DEADLIEST CATCH

MATHEW KAUFMAN

The Fishing Vessel Northern Light: The crew had been on a mission to head back to port for the last twelve hours. They discovered their gear ravaged by crab. Something that none of them have ever seen before.

Nets shredded, crab mangled or altogether missing, and the bait bags destroyed. The equipment was unserviceable, and they needed repairs before the season could continue. Something wasn't adding up... Welcome aboard.

January 10th, 1987
Dutch Harbor
The Bering Sea
F/V Northern Light

Forklifts drove up and down the docks delivering loads of fish, food, and equipment to the docked vessels. The smell of diesel fuel and fresh salt water twisted through the air. Seagulls screeched and landed atop the docked boats.

Captain Rich Johnson stood from his chair in the wheelhouse. The crew had been packing on a new load of bait for the last three hours. The crab had been incredibly voracious and more cunning than usual this year.

Normally the crew would grind the bait, pack it in a pouch, and hang it in the pot along with freshly carved up codfish. That had been the way he and all the other crab vessels had always done it. It was simple and it worked. This year was different. When some of the pots were hauled up, the netting around them was shredded, the bait bags emptied, and the crabs missing.

That didn't sit well with the veteran captain. He'd never seen anything like it, and it just didn't seem right. It almost looked like giant claw marks. Like Freddy Krueger ripped them up. What could do that kind of damage? Sharks? Maybe. Not likely.

Maybe it was a harder winter this year. Food at the bottom of the sea may be scarcer than normal. But that doesn't sit right either. Why would they shred the pots? A problem for another time.

"Hey Cap, we are about ready to shove off again. Pots are repaired and the bait is stocked," Kagen said.

"Right, then. Send a ring when the lines are pulled and we can push back," Rich said.

"Aye, Captain, a ring I'll be sendin'," Kagen said as he disappeared below.

"Jesus, Kagen, can you stop talking like a pirate? Shit drives me nuts!"

"No can do, Captain. I been doin' it so long I can't. Plus, it be bringin' us some luck, it be!"

"Damnit man, it's not even good pirate-speak. Whatever, just go do it somewhere else," the captain said.

It really did bug the hell out of him, but fishermen are a strange bunch to begin with. Not to mention Kagen was one of the best deck bosses he'd ever seen. The man could fish circles around any other crewman in the fleet.

A few minutes later the bell rang, alerting him it was time. Rich stood and stretched his body left and right, loosening up his muscles and stiff joints. The sea was a bitch to a man's body and the last thirty years of sailing on them had not been gentle.

His aches faded as the captain made a round through the wheelhouse, verifying the boat was ready. The stack of pots was chained. The crew was coiling the mooring lines, and the ship was free.

With a turn of the key and a stroke of his thick white beard, the dual engines rumbled to life down below. The ship's hull vibrated. Various electronics beeped and whirred as they powered on. The captain retrieved the microphone and gave the button a couple clicks before he spoke.

"Hold tight all, were setting off. Get some rest before we reach the fishin' grounds," Rich said.

The men on deck nodded, some tossed a thumbs up to acknowledge him. Somewhere down below he heard the pirate affirmative, making him cringe. He loved this part. Setting out to sea. Just his boat, his men, and himself. The sea was truly one of nature's last unexplored frontiers. Clear of the docks, he throttled up and steamed his way out of port and into the vast Bering Sea.

Early evening approached as the Northern Light reached the fishing grounds. The seas were tranquil, nary a wave to be seen. Captain Rich's stomach growled as the smell of dinner wafted up from down below.

His wife hated being away from him while he spent

months at sea. She'd begged for him to let her go along, insisting she could be useful on the ship. He'd argued endlessly at first. *Women don't belong on a boat. The sea is too dangerous. The men—they won't be able to stop looking at you. You're too beautiful.*

The last one was the line of bullshit that cost him the arguments. Not that she wasn't beautiful. She was in her mid-thirties but looked like a twenty-year-old. A slender five and a half feet tall, blond hair, big... Well, you get the point. She was gorgeous and the love of his life, and clearly better at arguing than he was. Her presence on the ship proved that.

The worst part was that she ended up being very useful. She cooked and cleaned for the crew. Did laundry, swept, mopped, and scrubbed anything that needed it. A master of women's work. She even made his bed and brought him coffee. A fine woman indeed.

Rich's stomach growled loud enough he could hear it over the engines. He pulled back on the throttle and the ship idled down. One more deep inhale of the deliciousness cooking below deck had him on his feet and yelling down the stairs.

"Hey, Vicky, how much longer 'til dinner is ready? I'm starving," Rich said.

"Putting it out on the table now," she yelled back. "Do you want yours up there or are you able to come down for dinner?"

"I'll be right down," he yelled. His feet were faster than his mouth. He was three steps down before he finished the reply.

Kagen was seated at the table already with something dark covering an eye... As he got closer the object was easily identifiable. *An eye patch.*

"God damnit! Get that fucking eye patch off. What the hell is wrong with you? Just when I think you can't get any more ridiculous than you already are, you find a way to make it even worse," Rich said.

"But Captai..."

"No. Not another word. I swear to God. I will drag you outside, grind you up, and use *you* as crab bait," the captain threatened.

"Oh, Rich, it looks good on him. It's very becoming of him. Plus, it makes the men laugh," Vicky said as she set down the final plates.

"No! And don't you encourage his bullshit. You can be bait too, woman," Rich said.

Vicky looked at Kagen and smiled, "I think he might be serious. You should probably take it off."

Reluctantly, Kagen removed the eye patch and began laughing.

"What? Do I even want to know?" Rich asked.

The other deck hands were sitting down at the table now. Each had a smile on their faces. Kagen's nonsense was really amusing to them. He didn't get it though. It was so dumb.

"Of course, you want to know, Captain. It's great news!" Kagen exclaimed.

"Oh, God... What?" he said, knowing something stupid was coming.

"Captain, I can—I can *SEA* better!" Kagen said, delivering a wink to everyone at the table. "Get it? SEA? It's like SEE. But SEA!"

Rich rolled his eyes, "You really are the worst." The jokes this guy came up with were horrible. He couldn't imagine what it was like being trapped in his head. "You're going to pay for this crap. I promise."

Everyone else laughed at the exchange. But the conversation quieted quickly as the food was served and devoured. Mashed potatoes smothered in butter, steak seared to perfection, green beans greened to goodness.

"Save a little for me," Vicky said.

"No promises, ma'am," Kyle Horn, the newest member of the crew, said. "It's delicious. I haven't had food this good since before my mom passed."

The kid had explained to Rich when he'd interviewed that he was here to find himself and prove that he could handle being out on his own. His dad was never in his life and his mom died a month and a half ago.

Kyle had a little brother, Tim or Tommy or something, that went to live with his aunt, but she was too poor to keep him without help. So that was just another reason he was here. He would do anything for his little brother and that included working a crab boat as a greenhorn on the Bering Sea.

"You poor boy," Vicky said. "All alone out here with this crew of misfits and Captain Cranky. Don't let 'em push you around too much."

"No, ma'am. I won't," Kyle said. A quiver of nervousness in his voice.

"Call me Vicky. I insist."

"The hell he will. He'll continue to call you ma'am until I can figure out if he's worth a shit and doesn't get us all killed or dragged to the bottom of the sea." Rich said.

"Yes, sir," Kyle replied.

"To Davey Jones' Locker, you mean" Kagen interrupted.

"That's enough. Get your no-good asses dressed and back on deck," Rich ordered.

The crew chuckled at the joke as they left the galley. Vicky handed Rich a steaming cup of coffee and gave him a kiss. About to head up stairs, Rich realized that Joe wasn't there. His stomach had clearly clouded his mind.

"Where's Joe?" he asked Vicky.

"Oh, he's having some stomach problems. I'll save you the details. Something about muddy like a back road in Kentucky. I don't remember the whole thing, but it was gross."

"Okay, then... thanks. He has a few extra minutes to eat if he thinks he can stomach it. We're gonna be half an hour or so before we reach the grounds."

"I'll let him know," Vicky said. "But he wasn't looking so hot."

"I hope it's nothing serious. I can't have everyone shitting the boat," Rich said.

Just then Kagen burst back into the galley and yelled, "You mean... the poop-deck!" before disappearing just as fast as he arrived.

"Fuck this..." Rich said as he returned to the wheelhouse.

January 10th, 1987
65 miles NW of St. Paul Island
The Bering Sea
F/V Northern Light

BEEP! The speaker blurted a notice, signaling the launch of the next pot. The hydraulics of the launcher hummed to life, tipping and causing the thousand-pound steel crab pot to slide off and plunge into the sea. Water splashed as the metal submerged before sinking quickly. Two buoys followed in quick succession, marking the pot for easy later retrieval.

The seas were rising now. The boat bobbed up and down in the water. Night had set in, and the men were fighting the freezing spray under the bright white sodium deck lights. Rich listened to the sounds of the deck through the open mic down there.

"Horn! Hurry the hell up. I gotta shit," Joe said. "I will do it in your bunk if you keep falling behind on bait."

"Yes, sir," the obviously tired greenhorn replied.

Rich had noticed him slowing down over the past hour and a half. Nothing unusual for a new guy. This would be the first of many times he'd need to decide if he was going to quit or dig deep and finish up this string of bait.

Rich watched as the boy ground bait and filled bags between sets. He quickly sprinted to each pot and baited them. Rich remembered his first fishing trip on a crab boat. It was hell. But this was the worst season to start in.

Opilio crab season started in January. That was one of the worst months to be on the Bering Sea. Cold temperatures, freezing ocean spray, flu season, rising seas, floating ice packs. The reasons go on and on.

He had to give it to the kid. Kyle was toughing it out better than he would have. Shit, he'd had 'horns that quit the first or second day and barely did half the work this kid was doing. Work ethics were really lacking with the new generation. But this kid, so far at least, was an exception.

That was good; he hated getting new deckhands. The cycle of training the same things over and over. The same problems, the same hassles. Typical shit. Hopefully not with this one.

Rich picked up the microphone, "Last one."

The crew picked up the pace slightly, obviously excited to get off deck, get some rest, and recover some before they had to haul all the pots. At least the money was good. Rich new guys who worked four months a year and took the other eight off.

What a life. *BEEP*. He signaled for the final time this string. The pot splashed into the sea. Bouy, buoy, and a collective sigh.

"Come on in, fellas. Get warm and get some sleep."

"I gotta shit! Get out of the way," Joe yelled as he clenched his cheeks together and hurried off deck.

"Aye, Captain, time to rech*arrr*ge." Kagen said.

Rich switched off the deck mic. That was enough of that shit. He never quits. What a weirdo.

January 11th, 1987
70 miles NW of St. Paul Island
The Bering Sea
F/V Northern Light

"Haul it!" the captain said over the loudspeaker as the first set of buoys came into sight. He clicked on the deck mic so he could hear what was going on.

Kagen threw the hook, snagged the line, and placed it into the block. The machine whirred to life as it pulled the sunken crab pot from the freezing depths. Round and round the rope spun in the coiler.

"Here we go boys, this is it," Joe said. "Let's hope nothing trashed these pots."

"Let's hope not. I kinda like the doubloons these crabs bring in," Kagen said.

"You really are a weirdo. Don't you think ol' Kagen is a weirdo, 'horn?" Joe asked.

"I don't—"

"That's right, 'horn. You don't have an opinion, if you know what's good for ye," Kagen said.

The captain clicked the mic, "Shut the hell up and pull the damn pot, would ya?"

"You're no fun, Cap!" Kagen yelled.

The top of the pot emerged from the freezing sea. The crew pulled it from the water with the ship's crane. It was stuffed with crab. Even with just the short soak it was still packed.

The crew emptied the pot onto the sorting table and counted it.

"Two hundred and forty-seven, cap. Two. Four. Seven," Joe yelled to the speaker.

"Copy. Two. Four. Seven," The captain repeated.

The crew of the Northern Light continued to haul pots up and send them back down for the remainder of the day. The captain knew better than to leave good fishing grounds for the possibility of more crab elsewhere.

The cycle of pull and drop had been going for several hours. The captain checked his maps. One last string. This last string was close to...

A loud bang below deck stopped the captain mid-thought. He froze for a moment and just listened. The ship developed a shimmy. He shook in his chair.

Quickly he grabbed the throttle and pulled back. He reached for the mic as the tremor subsided. He clicked the mic and held it to his mouth.

"I got a shimmy up here. You hear that bang, too?" he asked the crew.

"Yeah, cap," Kagen said with a noticeable lack of pirate bullshit.

"Head below deck and figure out what the hell is going on," the captain ordered.

"You want us to finish this pot in the block first or head down?" Kagen asked.

"Screw the crab. We need to figure out what the crash was."

He turned off the engines and watched as the men scrambled below deck. The speaker in the wheelhouse hummed with eerie silence. The captain watched from his perch and the vessel bobbed in the open water.

He hoped there was nothing wrong with the ship. They were over seventy miles from help, and it only took minutes for a ship to sink into the freezing water. Sure, they had survival suits, but he'd lost a ton of friends to the Bering Sea.

The seas had been picking up all afternoon and now, as darkness was settling in, he couldn't afford to lose an engine in the rising seas. He sat back and took a deep breath. *No sense in panicking now.*

Another boom broke the silence. This time it was over the speaker from the deck. Probably just the pot slamming into the side of the ship.

He stared at the rope... It moved to and fro with the movement of the ship. He continued to watch. Nothing. No more noises either.

Rich leaned back and took a deep breath. The tension was so thick he could almost cut it. The crew had only been below for a couple minutes but from the wheelhouse it felt like hours. Not knowing what was going on definitely didn't help.

Movement caught the captain's eye. There, just off the starboard side, next to the rope holding the pot. Something dark. It was hard to see what it was. He squinted and focused harder.

Something was there. It was definitely moving. It even flopped over on the rail a few times and wrapped around the metal. *What the hell?*

"Vicky! Vicky! Get up here, now!" Rich yelled, never looking away.

He heard his wife ascending the stairs.

"What is it? Is everything okay?"

"Do you see that?" he said, pointing.

"See what? Where is everyone?" she asked.

"Right there. Off the side. Right next to the launcher. That dark thing. Watch. It will move."

Just as he said, they saw movement. It looked like it was trying to gain traction on the rail. *Was it a man overboard from another ship? No, that's crazy. No one could survive in the freezing water. Not without a survival suit, and those were bright orange.*

"I see it. What is it?" Vicky asked?

"How the hell would I know? I just asked *you* what it was. Jesus Christ..."

"Where is everyone?" Vicky asked again.

"Below deck. There was a bang and a shimmy, and I sent them down to check what was going on," Rich said, turning to his wife.

When he looked back outside, the deck was empty. No odd shapes, nothing visible anywhere. *Where did it go?*

"It's gone. What the hell?" Rich said. "Will you do me a favor and run out there and just see what you see? Be careful, it's getting icy, but the ship isn't moving."

"Yes! I want to know what it was, too!" she said.

She was gone in a flash. Her feet clattering down the steps. Rich heard the bulkhead open and close as his wife stepped onto deck. A few seconds later she came into view.

Slipping and sliding in her tennis shoes, she made her way to the launcher where the shape had been. Touching the icy steel, she peered overboard. Rich watched her lean further.

"Be careful," he said over the speaker. "Do you see anything?

He wife stood and turned toward the wheelhouse.

"No. I can't see anything. It's dark," she said.

"There's a flashlight right there. Next to the coiler."

It was darker now than when the men went below. He could still see the rope off the side, but objects were starting to appear as dark outlines. He'd love to fire up the sodium lights, but they required the engines to be running for the generators to be powered. Only minimal electronics worked off battery power, and his crew had to turn off the generators in order to investigate the tremor.

His wife clicked on the flashlight and slid her way back to the rail. Again, she peered over the side and swung the light around, searching for whatever had been moving.

"I still don't see anything," she said.

"Okay, can you go see what the boys found so far and let me know?" Rich asked.

"Yep," she replied.

He watched his wife turn away and start walking across the deck. Something banged against the ship again and, this time, a dark object flipped over the top and a large shadow appeared as it slipped aboard.

"Vicky!" Rich yelled, forgetting to click the mic.

His wife was nearly to the door. She had to have heard whatever that was flop onto the deck. He fumbled for the mic. Click.

"Vicky!" he yelled again. This time she heard it and spun around toward his voice.

A blackish-green figure appeared, now illuminated by the flashlight. His wife screamed as she saw the creature behind her.

It was shaped like a man. It had arms and legs but was covered in scales. She stood there and stared at the creature and continued to scream. Rich could see the creature moving toward her. He pushed the throttle to make the ship lunge, hoping to knock them off balance and save his wife from whatever this was. Nothing happened. He forgot it was off.

He turned the key and pressed the starter. Nothing. The boys must have flipped a breaker below. *Shit.*

He did the only thing he could think of doing and ran down the stairs and headed for the deck. Screams echoed through the passages. He burst onto the deck. At the other end he heard the crew clamoring out as well.

"Captain?" They yelled in the darkness. "Is someone screaming?"

"Vicky! It has Vicky!" he yelled back.

The crew and captain met in the middle of the deck, colliding. Rich fell on his ass with a solid, whump.

"Sorry, cap, "Joe said. "Who has Vicky? What are you talking about?"

"Something came aboard. It came from the sea. Some kind of monster. I don't... I don't know," the captain said.

"You're screwing with us, right?" Joe said.

"I saw it. We gotta find Vicky," Rich said. "Did you turn the power on? Find anything wrong?"

"We didn't see anything wrong in the engine room. But the drive shaft was flamin' hot," Kagen reported.

"Okay, I'm gonna go fire up the boat and turn on the

sodiums. Stay here and listen for Vicky. I'll be right back. Grab something to beat the shit out of the monster with."

Rich ran back to the wheelhouse as fast as he could. By the time he got to his chair he was out of breath and panicked. He reached for the key, turning it with his shaking hand. He pressed the starter and the engines roared to life.

He flipped the switch to the sodium light and, thirty seconds later, the deck was illuminated as bright as day. He searched for Vicky, but she was nowhere to be seen. He picked up the mic.

"I'm gonna get the shotgun out of the safe. Start searching for her. I'll be there soon," Rich said.

"Yes, sir" the crew replied in unison. They split up and began the search.

Rich ran to his stateroom and uncovered the gun safe. He fudged the combo twice before it opened. The Winchester Model 1897 stood inside. It was a Vietnam era "trench gun." It had been passed down from his grandfather and kept on the boat for protection from a mutiny.

Rich checked the weapon to make sure it was loaded. All six shells were there and one was even in the chamber. In the corner of the safe was a box of shells. He grabbed a handful and tossed them in the pocket of his jeans and started for the deck.

He figured there was no way the creature had made its way back to this end of the ship. Rich hadn't seen it pass him and Vicky surely would have screamed. Once on deck he removed a key from his pocket and locked the bulkhead door to this end of the ship.

He stepped back out onto the deck. He pulled the

shotgun up to the ready and clicked the safety off. He took a long deep breath to calm his nerves and hopefully prevent him from accidentally shooting Vicky or a member of his crew should they appear in front of his barrel.

The freezing wind swept across his exposed face. *Should have grabbed a jacket.*

Who would think logically when someone steals the one person in this world you love? They didn't have kids. Living practically year-round on a boat was prohibitive of that. He certainly didn't want to get caught having sex with his wife by a bunch of horny fishermen. The crabs they caught from the sea were the only crabs he wanted on the boat.

Rich crossed the deck. When he reached the far side, past the holding tanks that separated the underdecks, he headed below.

This was it. It was pitch dark and there was some sort of goddamn monster down there that took his bride. Who was going to cook dinner? Who would take care of him when he was sick? Who would accompany him to parties?

He intended to ensure that the answer, the only answer, was Vicky. No fucking sea "thing" was going to stop that. Not if he has a say, anyway.

Rich took the steps one at a time as he entered the ship. The sounds of the howling wind and breaking seas were quickly replaced by the thundering beats of his heart pounding in his chest.

He couldn't even hear the slop of his wet boots touching the metal steps. But still he listened intently for any sounds that might reveal the location of the monster or Vicky. So far, nothing.

Thump-thump. Thump-thump. Thump-thump. Thump-thump. His heart pounded in quick succession.

Reaching the bottom, Rich found himself enveloped in darkness. *Shit. No fucking flashlight.*

It was too late to go back now. He's come too far to turn back and risk Vicky. She was his everything. The only one that put up with him.

"Vicky!" he whispered as loud as he dared. "Vicky, where are you? Call out if you can hear me."

Silence. There were only so many places they could be down here. There were the generator room and the forward holds, sealed by bulkhead doors that make noisy creaks when you open or close them. He doubted they'd be in there. Lastly, there were the forward storage rooms, two of them, not to mention the corridors.

But why did he take Vicky? The only reason he can think of is convenience. *Thud! Bang!* The sound of an object bouncing off sheet metal broke the rhythm of his pounding heart.

"HELP!" Vicky screamed. "I'm..."

His bride's voice was silenced. Rich raised the shotgun and started slowly down the hallway. Everything was metal around him. There was no way to tell exactly where they were. Too much echo. Too much darkness.

Step, step, step. One foot in front of the other. Rich was careful not to cross his feet and trip himself. That would be a stupid way to die.

The shotgun was heavy, but adrenaline is a hell of a drug. He knew he couldn't hold the gun up forever. There was very little chance of this lasting forever though. Someone was likely going to die. Maybe several someones. He just hoped it was the creature that took Vicky.

He creeped his way around each corner, slowly advancing, anxiously awaiting the moment a shootable target appeared at the business end of his rifle.

Left corner, then right. He reached the center of the ship's bow section where a three-way intersection awaited. He had a fifty-fifty chance that if the brute was there, he'd have turned the wrong way. If that happened there was no way out. Death would come for him expeditiously.

Another scream escaped his wife. She was closer now. Ten feet? Fifteen? Close. He chose the hallway to the left, almost sure that's where the sound came from.

He opened his eyes wide as wide as he could, straining to see anything. Shades of darkness filled his vision. Grays and blacks melded together.

"Rich, I'm here!" Vicky screamed. The panic was evident in her voice. He was running out of time, and he knew it.

He gripped the shotgun and spun around the corner. The barrel struck something. He recoiled in fear. Something pushed back the barrel and jerked it. This caused the weapon to discharge with an ear shattering crack. His ears rang and his eyes lost their night vision, now useless from the bright muzzle flash.

Rich racked the rifle; the foregrip slid back and forth, chambering another round. His ears buzzed with canned lightning. *There. I think I see it moving.*

"Mlent hner gno!" Rich yelled out, his voice muffled and practically unintelligible.

More movement. He fired again. This time he knew he'd missed as a brief flash of the creature and its claws appeared.

It was too late. His eyes couldn't focus fast enough to dodge the attack. A searing pain spread across his chest as it clawed him.

He could feel the warm liquid spreading across his chest. He knew he'd been hit. The thing had clawed his chest and now he was bleeding. He just didn't know how bad.

What he did know was that Vicky wasn't with this sea creature when he pulled the trigger. He didn't see her at all in the brief illumination. He raised the gun again, racking in a fresh shell.

He fired. Bang! Another miss followed by a claw slash. This time against his forearm. He knew it was deep when his pinky and ring finger stopped working. Something critical for moving them had been hit.

He managed to rack the weapon again and fired when the shadow moved... Rack. Pull. Bang.

He fired several more shots. He knew he registered a hit when a splash of cold liquid struck him. It was followed by another as a consecutive round struck the creature. He advanced to where he'd last seen the it and tripped, colliding hard with the wall and slumping to the floor in a puddle of wetness, both warm and cold. Their blood mixed on the floor.

"Vicky?" Rich yelled.

No answer.

"Anyone? Joe? Kagen?" He couldn't remember the new kids name...

It didn't matter. He had to get the lights on. To do that, he'd have to flip the breaker. His chest burned from its new wounds. The breaker was close. He had to get there. Had to find Vicky. Had to find his crew. Had to staunch this bleeding.

He stood up, dropping the shotgun on the way to his feet. Stumbling and using the wall for support, he shuffled to the breaker box, searching the walls with each step.

He forced himself to open the box and fumbled for the switches before flipping them one at a time. Bit by bit, light after light illuminated, bringing the horrific scene into view. The creature lay in a pool of its own black blood.

"NO!" he screamed.

Next to the scaly brute, sharing the same blood pool, was Vicky. Her red blood now intertwined with the creatures. Swirls of black and red. Both leaking their life out onto the cold metal floor.

He rushed to her and rolled her over. *This can't be. She wasn't there.* But what was there was the gaping hole in her chest. He knew it was the work of a shotgun, but how? He hadn't seen her. She wasn't there and he knew it.

He felt for a pulse. Nothing. She was gone. All that remained was her lifeless body. The husk of a person. His wife. Vicky.

The shock had subsided enough for Rich to return to the wheelhouse. Kagen, somehow, joined him minutes later as he throttled up the engines. He looked at Kagen.

"The others didn't make it," Kagen said. No hint of pirate-speak.

Rich's left arm hung by a thread of meat and a belt stopped the stump from bleeding. He knew he should say something. Instead, he returned his focus to the controls.

The shimmy that had caused the vessel to stop in the first place returned. Rich didn't care and pushed the lever further forward. Shimmy turned into shakes. Shakes turned into rattles and before long smoke billowed up from below.

"There's a fire, cap," Kagen said. "Probably from the driveshaft. It was hot before and you're pushing hard. We gotta shut it down and radio for help."

Rich remained silent and steered the vessel toward St.

Paul Island, seventy miles away. The smoke grew thicker by the minute. In minutes, flames peeked up from below deck.

The two remaining crew members glanced at each other and exchanged a look of knowing. There was no surviving this. They were as good as dead. Fire or freezing water. Both raced toward them and it didn't matter which one.

Death was death.

WEREWOLF PORNO

JEFF STRAND

"*Fluffer!*"

Carl watched the silicone-enhanced blonde let out an annoyed sigh, shove a bookmark into her copy of *Women Who Do Too Much*, and walk across the set. Without a word she knelt down in front of Teddy "Third-Leg" Tracer and went to work.

This was Carl's first time on the set of an adult motion picture, and he was still getting used to the fact that people could be standing around looking bored while an attractive woman performed oral sex. Most of them weren't even watching! He wanted to shout "Hey, you jaded idiots, there's a hot chick in a thong bikini giving a blowjob here! What the hell is your problem? Gape, already!"

Even Teddy didn't seem all that interested in what was happening below his waist. Carl, who had never gotten oral pleasure that didn't receive his 100% undivided attention, wanted to slap the guy with one of the strap-ons that had been used in the previous scene.

"Let's go, let's go!" shouted the director, Garry Ecks. "Time is money!"

The fluffer pulled her mouth away from Teddy, which took a moment. "If you're in such a big hurry, *you* suck it."

Garry ignored the comment and turned his attention to the lead actress. "Darla, dammit, if you don't quit moving I'm going to weld your knees to that mattress! We're on a tight schedule here!"

Darla Duncan was one of the rising stars of the adult entertainment world. She was nineteen years old and had skyrocketed to fame after starring in the incredibly popular reality porn series *Darla Dares*, where she'd pick up random guys off the street and perform whatever acts they dared her to do (they were usually naughty). Less than half an hour ago, Carl had learned that the "random" guys were in fact paid actors and that the entire series was completely scripted. A little bit of light had faded from his world.

Darla was currently on her hands and knees on the bed. She shifted positions long enough to give Garry the finger. He glared at her, glared at a few random crew members for no apparent reason, then glared at Teddy. "Are you ready yet?"

Teddy gave him a thumbs-up sign. "Hard as molten steel, baby."

"Molten steel is melted steel, dipshit," said the fluffer.

"No, it's not. It's rock-hard steel."

"No, it's steel in liquid form. In times of yore, black-smiths would pour it into molds to create weapons and tools for use by the populace."

Teddy frowned. "Huh?"

"Goddammit, stop confusing my star!" Garry shouted.

"Since when the fuck is *he* the star?" Darla demanded.

"Enough!"

"It's my name selling DVDs, not his!"

"I said enough!

Teddy put his hand on the fluffer's head and chuckled. "Here, babe, create my weapon for use by the...uh..."

"Put your hand on me again and I'll gnaw your dick off."

"Enough! Enough! Enough! Enough! Enough! Enough! Enough! Enough! Enough! Enough!" Garry's face looked almost fluorescent red and Carl worried that his brains might pop out of his head like a money shot. "We're on a tight schedule here and we don't have time for this! Teddy, are you good to go or not?"

"My weapon is ready, baby."

"Then get on the goddamn bed! You need to get in there, come, and get out so we can set up the orgy! Is everybody ready to go? You all damn well better be ready to go! *Action*!"

Teddy climbed on the bed behind Darla, grabbed her by the hips, and thrust his extremely ample manhood into her. They went at it for a few moments until Garry shouted "*Cut*!"

"Cut? What do you mean, cut?" asked Darla.

"Could you please try to pretend that you're getting some pleasure out of this? He's not defragmenting your hard drive, he's screwing you! Act like you're getting screwed! Put on your 'I'm getting screwed' face, for fuck's sake!"

"Should I pull out?" asked Teddy.

"Yes! Pull out! We're gonna start over!"

Teddy withdrew and got off the bed. Darla gave Garry the finger again.

"Keep it up and by this time tomorrow you'll be turning twenty-dollar tricks at the geriatric ward," said Garry. "Are we still taping? Let's go, let's go, let's go! Teddy, are you ready?"

"Hell yeah. I'm gonna defragment her hard drive, baby."

"You are *such* a dumbass," the fluffer informed him.

"Shut up, everyone! *Action*!"

Teddy got back on the bed and re-entered Darla. Carl

didn't notice any real change in her demeanor, but Garry seemed satisfied and stopped shouting for a few minutes.

Jeez, he's good, Carl thought as Teddy pounded into her over and over at a staggering pace. God, and he had at least three inches on Carl, possibly four. (Carl didn't have a ruler handy, nor was he willing to endure the socially awkward situation of asking Teddy to submit to a measurement, particularly when his penis was busy.) The first tremors of performance anxiety started to form in the pit of his stomach.

Garry had assured him that his lack of a gargantuan phallus was okay, and that he wouldn't be expected to go at it like a seasoned porn star. "You'll just lie there; she'll do all the work," the director had explained. "As long as the moon does the trick, we'll have ourselves the ultimate porno flick, a bestiality masterpiece beyond anything the world has ever seen!"

Carl was a werewolf. Once a month, on the night of the full moon, he'd lock himself in his basement, transform into a snarling, howling beast, scrape the hell out of the concrete walls, and then return to human form by morning. He always took precautions and he'd never killed anybody, not even the neighbor's cat. He'd been bitten three years ago, during a camping trip that had been rather pleasant and relaxing until the gory werewolf attack. Though the first few months had been kind of rough, these days it was really not much more than a minor inconvenience, sort of like menstruation.

Of course, referring to menstruation as a "minor inconvenience" was why he was single these days. Still, he stood by his comparison.

Several weeks ago, he'd been laid off when his job at the insurance company's call center was outsourced to India.

He'd been working there seven years, since he was eighteen, and it was the only full-time job he'd ever held. Devastated, he'd wandered around the city for a while, hoping that upbeat music on his iPod would lift his spirits. It didn't, so he decided to get really drunk instead.

In the bar, he'd met Garry Ecks. They'd chatted for a while about how much life sucked. Carl had never met a genuine pornographer before but was too embarrassed to ask most of the questions on his mind, though he did inquire if the cameramen ever had to wear protective raingear (no).

As Carl officially drank one more beer than he should have, he said "Did I tell you I'm a werewolf?"

"Are you, now?" Garry looked amused.

"Yep." Carl held up his palm, revealing the pentagram.

"Damn. You carve that yourself?"

Carl shook his head. "It's real."

"So did they fire you for being a werewolf?"

"Nah, nobody at work knew. It only happens on the night of the full moon, but they'd probably have gotten all paranoid about me transforming during work hours and mauling the other employees and stuff."

"That could be a definite Human Resources issue."

"Not that it matters now, anyway," said Carl, shoving his half-empty bottle of beer aside. "I didn't even get a good severance package."

"I'm sure there are plenty of job opportunities for a lycanthrope," said Garry. "Maybe you could endorse a brand of hairball medicine."

"You don't believe me, do you?"

"Do you mean about the werewolf thing? Not really."

"Why would I lie about something like that?"

"You're drunk and desperate for attention."

Carl got off the wobbly stool and stood on wobbly legs. "I taped it once. I set the camera down in the basement and made a video of the whole thing. Well, not the *whole* thing— I sorta smashed up the camera after my transformation— but I salvaged the tape and I've got it at my apartment."

"Is that so?"

"Wanna see it?"

Garry stared at him for a long moment. Technically, three Garrys stared at him for a long moment with their six eyes, but Carl figured this was a side-effect of the alcohol.

"Sure."

They'd gone back to Carl's place. Carl popped the tape into the VCR and pressed play. An image of Carl kneeling on the floor of the basement appeared on the television screen. He was wearing a t-shirt and white boxer shorts.

"Usually I'm naked," he explained. "It doesn't make sense to put on clothes that are just going to get shredded when I transform. But I didn't want to be naked on the tape, you know, in case I ever sold this to television or anything, I didn't want them to have to blur out anything, and I also thought that it would, you know, be kind of embarrassing to have lots of people watch a video where you can see every-thing. Not that you would mind—I mean, you see naked guys all the time, I guess, not that I'm hitting on you or anything, I'm just babbling because I'm intoxicated, but anyway—"

"Let's just watch the video," Garry said.

"Yes, sir."

Carl fast-forwarded through a few minutes of him just sitting there, letting the tape resume when he began to twitch on-camera. "See, that's where the full moon is starting to affect me."

"Moonlight doesn't need to shine right on you?"

"Nope. It happens right at midnight."

"Ah. Good to know."

Garry frowned as the tape showed Carl falling into the fetal position. As the first strands of black fur formed on Carl's chest, Garry flinched. Carl grinned an inebriated grin as the pornographer leaned closer to the television screen, watching every detail of Carl's transformation. He thrashed around, screaming in pain as fangs grew, bones changed shape, and body hair sprouted like puberty gone terribly wrong. Within two minutes he was a full wolf. The last image was of his jaws closing over the camera lens.

"Holy shit!" said Garry, jumping to his feet. "That wasn't CGI! I know CGI, and that wasn't it! You're a werewolf!"

"Duh, that's what I said."

"Oh my God, oh my God, oh my God, this is incredible! This is amazing! You're not going to mutilate me, are you?"

Carl shook his head. "Full moon's not for another two weeks."

Garry began to pace around the room. "I'm gonna make you a star. Forget the Paris Hilton and Pamela Anderson videos—this will be the greatest porn sensation of all time! Picture it: We get the hottest porn star in the business, and she fucks you—yes, you—while you turn into a werewolf!"

"I beg your pardon?"

"It will be the ultimate event in adult entertainment! The 'chicks doing dogs' audience will freak out over it, but the crossover potential is astounding!"

"I'm not a porn actor," Carl explained.

"Oh, but you will be!"

"I don't think I can do that."

"Yes, you can. You have a dick, right?"

Carl nodded.

"And you've inserted it into a vagina before, right?"

"I guess so."

"What do you mean, you guess so? That's an event that most people remember. It's one of the first things you see when you go south of the belly button. You can't miss it. You a virgin?"

"No, no, I've been with a couple of girls; I just don't have a lot of experience."

"A couple? Two?"

"Yeah."

"Just two?"

"Yeah."

"That's it?"

"Sorry."

"That's inhuman. You'd think you'd screw more women than that just by accident."

Carl shrugged.

"Are we talking two insertions total, or two long-term girlfriends? Or are you divorced?"

"Two sort-of long-term girlfriends."

"All right, I guess that makes sense," said Garry. "Well, no it doesn't, but whatever. This is gonna be fantastic. One unbroken shot. First, you're inside her as a man, then you're inside her as a wolf!"

"We can't do that," Carl insisted. "When I turn into a werewolf, the animal part completely takes over. I try to kill things."

"We probably shouldn't have you kill anybody; that's a whole different sub-genre. We'll just strap you down. Muzzle you. It'll play to the BDSM audience."

"I don't know..."

"You're unemployed, aren't you?"

"Yeah, but I was thinking about applying at Prudential or something."

"Prudential won't squash Darla Duncan's tits against your face. We are going to make adult film history, Carl. Werewolf porn. How the hell can you top that?"

And now Carl was on the movie set, waiting nervously for his big scene. He'd turned Garry down that night, and the following day, and the day after that. But Garry kept increasing the money offer...and it was Darla Duncan! Carl had spent many a lonely night over the past year pretending that his hand was Darla's mouth, and now he'd be with her for real.

"Ooooooooohhhhhhhhhh," Teddy moaned, pulling out and proving that his orgasm was the work of a method actor.

"Cut!" shouted Garry. "Teddy, good job. Darla, get yourself cleaned up for the next scene."

"Yeah, yeah, whatever."

"All right, let's get Carl in his restraints and get the orgy people in here! Let's go, let's go, midnight is approaching!"

Suddenly Carl felt like he was going to throw up and wasn't sure if he could really go through with this. He wasn't a porn star. His pelvis couldn't thrust as rapidly as Teddy's.

"Right here," said one of the stagehands, beckoning him over. Carl reluctantly walked to his spot, wishing that he'd never gotten drunk, had never shown off the werewolf tape, had never agreed to appear in a porno flick, and had never walked over to the spot where the stagehand beckoned him.

A line of attractive and extremely naked people, five men and five women, walked onto the set. Carl wasn't entirely sure of the plot significance (it was not a tightly constructed screenplay), but they'd all be having sex in the background as part of some sort of ritual, while Darla rode him in the foreground during the transformation.

"Strip 'em off," the stagehand said, pointing to Carl's boxers.

"Now?"

"Uh, yeah. These days, they try to include nudity in porn films."

"You don't have to be sarcastic." Carl removed his boxers and stood there naked, hoping that nobody was staring at his inferior genitalia. He listened for telltale snickers but heard none.

"On your back," said the stagehand.

Carl lay on the mattress, which was covered with red sheets that in some way figured into whatever the ritual was (again, the screenplay was not totally clear on this issue). Three more guys joined the stagehand, and they quickly chained Carl's arms and legs to the floor. The wrist and ankle bands were made out of some kind of rubber that would stretch to fit his werewolf proportions at the appropriate time but would not allow him to pull free.

"Are you sure that's tight enough?" asked Darla, poking at one of the restraints with her toe.

"Don't worry, he's not going anywhere," the stagehand assured her.

"Orgy people! Start screwing!" Garry shouted. "We're ten minutes away!"

As the naked people began to touch, nibble, lick, and penetrate each other, the stagehand slid the protective mask over Carl's head. It was clear plastic, sort of shaped like a lopsided astronaut helmet, and would allow everybody to see Carl's head transform into a werewolf head while preventing him from biting Darla's face off.

"He's good to go," the stagehand announced.

"Perfect!" said Garry. "We've got five minutes! Darla, do your thing!"

"He's not hard."

"Carl, get hard!" Garry shouted.

"I'm not sure I can," Carl admitted.

"What the sweet fuck do you mean you're not sure you can? *Fluffer!*"

The fluffer sighed, marked her spot again, walked over, and knelt down next to Carl. She put her face in his lap and took him into her mouth.

Carl was so nervous that he could barely feel it. *Think hard thoughts. Steel towers. Concrete blocks. Guns. Anvils. Bananas...no, no, bananas are soft, you idiot! Think of marble statues. Trains.*

Or perhaps—here was a novel idea! —he could think about the blowjob-in-progress. That seemed like a much more efficient course of action.

"Goddamnit, I'm not seeing any bulges in your cheek!" Garry shouted.

The fluffer opened her mouth, and Carl's limp penis flopped back against his testicles. "Nothing's happening."

"So suck with more enthusiasm and skill! What the hell are we paying you for?"

The fluffer rolled her eyes and resumed her head-bobbing.

Relax...just relax...enjoy the way her tongue swirls with expert precision, despite her surly attitude...

"We're running out of time!" Garry screamed. "Get that thing in a fuckable state in the next thirty seconds or you'll never fluff in this town again!"

"You can't build the Empire State Building out of wet noodles," said the fluffer.

"It would actually kind of help if you didn't say things like that," Carl pointed out.

"Darla! Get down there and help out!"

"That's *her* job!"

"I don't give a rat's ass! We need a goddamn erection

here! Orgy ladies, get over there! Everybody, take a quadrant!"

Carl lay there, not quite able to believe that he now had several hot naked women running their tongues over him...and he couldn't get it up! He should have suspected that this would turn into a cruel joke. His penis had always hated him, and now it was wreaking its penile vengeance.

"What can I do?" Garry asked. "Would it help if Teddy went down there, too?"

"Hey!" Teddy protested. "I'm not queer!"

"You'll be queer if I tell you to! This is more important than your homophobia! We're making cinematic history here! Get over there and suck his cock!"

"I won't do it!"

"The hell you won't!"

"That won't help!" Carl insisted. "It'll make things worse; I promise. Lots worse."

He closed his eyes. *Relax...imagine that you're on a desert island, surrounded by naked women...*

He opened his eyes so he could better see the naked women that were right there. God, this was dumb.

"I felt a twitch!" one of the orgy ladies proclaimed.

"You mean it?" Garry asked.

"A definite twitch!"

"I felt it, too!" said the fluffer.

"Keep doing what you're doing! Don't lose the momentum!"

"It's growing! It's growing!"

"Perfect!" Garry rubbed his hands together in glee. "Orgy ladies—back to your original spots! It's almost midnight!"

As Darla and the fluffer continued to vigorously work on him, Carl grew and grew. Yes! Nothing cured impotence like seven female tongues!

"Fluffer! Get the hell out of the shot! We're gonna start filming!"

The fluffer left. Darla squatted on top of Carl and eased herself onto his mighty erection. It felt pretty darn good.

He'd expressed concerns about the upcoming size increase, but Garry had assured him that Darla could handle it. "Are you bigger than a fire extinguisher?" he'd asked.

"No."

"Then it's cool."

Carl lay there, watching Darla bounce, thinking that maybe he could get used to the porn star life, even without the whole werewolf angle.

"It's midnight!" Garry announced.

For a moment, Carl was too distracted by the feeling of being inside Darla Duncan to notice the familiar tingles. But then the tingles quickly turned to pain, and he helplessly watched his chest become much more hairy.

"Ooooh, baby, if I have to shave, so you do," said Darla, reading off a cue card.

Carl's nails extended and there was the usual agony as his bones began to change shape. Darla bounced faster.

She giggled as his penis transformed inside of her.

The band holding his right wrist snapped.

Oops...that's probably not good...

The band holding his left wrist snapped.

Bad...really, really bad...herpes bad...

He tried to call out a warning, but it came out as a growl.

Shit!

Darla was gasping with pleasure and thrusting so hard that she didn't seem to notice the major safety issue.

Is nobody paying attention? Any second now the wolf is gonna take over and—

Carl slammed his paws against Darla's head, jamming five claws into each side. She stopped bouncing as he twisted his paws, giving her a makeshift facial reconstruction. Blood poured onto his furry chest, and he could smell it even through the plastic mask.

Hungry...so hungry...

He released his grip on her head. Darla, still impaled upon him, slumped forward as Carl tore off the mask. Jaws free, he took a great big bite out of her face.

Lots of naked people screamed.

Garry figured his career was pretty much fucked as the werewolf pounced onto the orgy participants. The men's erections had all vanished, and within a few moments so had three of the five penises. He stared in shock as the werewolf rapidly mauled them, sending blood, chunks of flesh, and silicone implants flying into the air.

"Do something!" Teddy cried.

"What the hell do you want me to do?"

"Kill it! You're the director!"

"With what?"

Carl the Psycho Werewolf bit off somebody's arm, which looked like it really hurt. He swallowed it in two gulps.

"A silver bullet!"

"Did you bring one?"

"No! Why would *I* bring one?"

Garry cringed. One of the cutest asses in the porn business wasn't quite so cute anymore.

"I don't know! Foresight, maybe?"

"How could you be so irresponsible as to bring a live werewolf in here with no way to kill it?"

"It wasn't supposed to get away!"

"Well, it did!"

"I know that!"

Carl was dining on the intestines of one of the actresses. Garry thought of a really funny "eating her out" joke, and then felt guilty about it.

"So why weren't you prepared?" Teddy demanded.

"I was prepared! Just not prepared enough!"

"I'm gonna sue your ass!"

"Why are *you* gonna sue? You're not the one getting devoured!"

"Mental anguish!"

"Screw you!"

Garry had to admit, he did feel rather foolish for setting up this film shoot without bringing a way to terminate the werewolf if things got out of hand. But that was neither here nor there at this point.

"Did you even have insurance for this?" Teddy asked.

"Of course!" Garry lied.

Carl stepped over the corpses of the orgy participants, then rushed across the room and took down one of the stagehands. The stagehand wailed in terror and agony, but stopped when the werewolf tore out his throat.

BANG!

The werewolf howled and turned around, snarling.

BANG! BANG! BANG!

The fluffer fired three more shots into the creature. It let out a loud whimper and then flopped over on its side. Garry, Teddy, the fluffer, and the remaining living crew members stared at it for a long moment.

"Is it dead?" Teddy asked.

"Go kick it and see," the fluffer said.

Teddy did so. The werewolf wasn't dead. The fluffer fired

a shot into its heart, and then a mercy shot into Teddy's forehead, knowing that he wouldn't want to live without his leg.

The werewolf transformed back into human form. Carl lay dead on the floor, riddled with bullet holes. Garry couldn't help but feel a little bit sorry for the poor kid, but at least he'd gotten laid before he died. That's how Garry would've wanted to go.

"Well, that sucked," said Garry.

The fluffer sighed. "You think?"

"We...we don't have to spread word about my negligence, right? I mean, how was I supposed to know he was telling the truth about being a werewolf? I thought he was some whacko off the street."

"I think we can work out a deal," said the fluffer. "But you're cleaning up the mess."

Blood Orgy Rampage of the Werewolf, featuring the farewell performance of Darla Duncan, was the #1 bestselling underground DVD of the year.

RENFIELD'S JOURNAL

LANCE TAUBOLD

"Demand me nothing, what you know, you know.
From this time forth I will never speak word."

I spoke these words for the first time in 1604 at The Globe in London as the immortalized character Iago in Will Shakespeare's, *Othello*.

I would go on to portray this incomparable character numerous times over the years, as well as many other of Shakespeare's other, ostensible, villains with Lord Chamberlain's Men at The Globe until 1642, when the Long Parliament closed all the English theaters in the First English Civil War.

Alas, all good things must come to an end.

Or, perhaps not?

My vast knowledge and acting prowess stood me in good stead for what was to come in the years ahead, as I assumed role after role, onstage... and off.

My name is Renfield, and, to my knowledge, all of what I am to say is true.

But I digress. The year is 1897 and I reside at Doctor

Seward's Sanitarium outside of London proper, assuming (humbly) my greatest character: Renfield, the apocryphal lunatic!

All of my planning and hard work has come to fruition: Dracula is coming. My master and his fifty coffins of Transylvanian earth have arrived here at Whitby Harbor. Unfortunately, the ship ran aground, and the crew have all mysteriously disappeared. *Joy*! What brilliant tomfoolery. I trust my master has been sated by the crew.

I have enlisted the Whitby locals to transfer the coffins of earth to their new address, personally overseeing the delivery of coffin fifty.

It has taken the better part of four days for the transfer and to scuttle the ship.

My lackeys, Jonathan Harker and the aforesaid Doctor Seward, have been most amenable in aiding me in my goal, not denying that my vampiric hypnotic suggestion had a degree of assistance there.

Assuming another of my fluid characterizations, I enlisted Harker's aid in procuring a suitable castle here in England for my master. Then, subsequently, sent the gullible fool off to Transylvania to facilitate it all.

I must say, Harker has done admirably and in right time as well, belying the fact that he, with all haste, wished to return to his beloved fiancée, Mina Murray, a fine morsel if ever there was one. Decidedly, my master will also delight in the charms of her best friend, the delicious Lucy Westenra. I will have Harker bring them round this week to meet the new master of Carfax Castle.

And now the Count Dracula may take up residence and enjoy his reign here in the largest city in Europe, where so many of the downtrodden and forgotten can find their eternal resting place, aided by the sanguine nature of my master. I will serve him to the utmost of my capabilities in procurement for him. Many of the hapless victims residing at Seward's asylum deserve to shuffle off this mortal coil as well. With Seward as my willing factotum, my master's thirst will be more than assuaged.

This time all has been carefully planned. It has been a decade since my master and I had our last disastrous foray here...

London: Late Summer-1888

My role: The Austrian Count Von Sternen, delivering his cousin to his final resting place after succumbing to a mysterious plague-like disease, keeping me mostly to my cabin belowdecks. Hint of the plague well-managed to keep intercourse with others onboard to a minimum.

I had acquired a modest estate for our time to be spent in London, a short ride into the city proper.

We began our nightly sorties in the city, scouring the various neighborhoods, and after a week of this, with varying success, we came upon our E Dorado:

Whitechapel.

Land of the hopeless and helpless. Thousands of parasites waiting to be consumed, flourishing in the dead of night. My master's bloodlust (and my own) was fraught with need. The gutters flowed crimson with the blood of animal entrails, heightening our senses into a febrile frenzy.

It was August thirty-first. "I must feed, Renfield," my master said, his hands on my shoulders, shaking me with his abnormal strength, enough to shake an ordinary man to death.

"Yes, master," I managed to stutter, then noticed a cloaked figure heading toward us. "There, master." I pointed.

I backed up into the shadows of the alley and watched

my master approach the figure. My master mumbled something I took to be a greeting of a sort, then heard a reply.
"Me name's Polly, good sir."

My master uttered a response.

"I got's me a place around the corner here." Polly
pointed behind her.

My master raised his arm, and his cloak engulfed the
girl. He ushered her off around the corner. I followed at a
discreet distance, and as I turned the corner I heard the
most blood-curdling scream, which was abruptly cut off,
lasting a mere second or so.

I dashed into the nearest small building and entered the
first door I came upon. I opened the door to a squalid room,
for that is all it was, and beheld the carnage my master had
wrought in brief seconds. It was an abattoir. Polly's clothes
were shredded. Her flesh was shredded. My master's head
was firmly planted in her neck, draining her life.

This would not do. An idea began to formulate as I
recalled my years in Edinburgh...

In the early 1800s I found myself in Scotland, studying
with the renowned surgeon Robert Liston. Liston prided
himself on the expediency of his amputations. As his
assistant, he would often have me time his skills. I would
make sure to always feed before an operation to keep my
blood fever at bay.

Liston was the first surgeon to operate with anesthesia.
In my time with him I observed him operating with and
without; hence his swiftness with the amputations to avoid
excessive pain to the patient.

I would decline to call Liston a conscientious surgeon.
Haste seemed to be his primary goal. Modesty
notwithstanding, he would often speak of his two-and-a
half-minute leg amputation and his removal of forty-five

scrotal tumors in four minutes—one of his more cringe-worthy surgeries.

He operated on the poor as well as the rich, for which he was scorned by many of his peers. In his thick brogue, he would say to me, "The poor have just as much right to live as anyone. Aye, Renfield?"

I would nod solemnly and say "aye" in agreement. It never did to argue with the doctor.

Liston's nemesis, albeit, was infection, losing many patients postoperatively to hospital gangrene. This was something I was careful to avoid. If I fed on a patient with the poison from gangrene in their system, I would be violently ill in reaction. Accordingly, as Liston was fond of operating on the poor, his "successes" also provided me with an accommodating food source.

The doctor was also quite territorial, and in order for me to hone my own surgical skills with the blades, I would have to "suggest" to the good doctor that perhaps he should rest and not overwork himself while I tried my hand at a surgery. Liston, perhaps not so surprisingly, given his arrogant nature, proved harder than most to convince with my hypnotic suggestions.

But I was more than up for the challenge.

After a couple of years of surgeries, I felt that I was sufficiently skilled and bid the good doctor adieu. I wished him well and told him I wished to venture out on my own.

He did not take my notice well and proceeded to repudiate me as being ungrateful.

Robert Liston died at his home in 1847. It was reportedly an aneurism.

I recall the taste of his favorite Highland whisky in his blood...

. . .

I always carried a small surgical kit—compliments of the good doctor—and set to rectifying the mayhem my master had perpetrated on poor Polly.

It was one of my better vivisectional efforts, I must say. Performing the "surgery" had a two-fold benefit: It would—and did—confuse the police as to the identity of the perpetrator and would also distract to the true purpose behind the reason for the slattern's death. Genius.

Alas, our bloody spree was to be short-lived. (I do love a clever pun.) The "Jack the Ripper" murders became all the rage. A letter to the police, some "clues" left here and there, and we had manipulated the most-profound mystery in history! The consequence being that after the last "double murder," all focus and manpower was turned to capturing the elusive "Monster of Whitechapel."

We were forced to return to Transylvania.

Back in London, after our first week of settling in, that fool, Harker, decides to pay his respects to my master.

Albeit, all is not lost, for Harker has also brought his lovely fiancée, the comely Mina Murray and her even lovelier companion, Miss Lucy Westenra.

I know from the look in my master's eyes that the lovely Lucy will be a most tasty morsel for his unquenchable thirst. My master has always thrived on human blood, never the vermin I choose to indulge in in my role as the "lunatic" Renfield at the asylum. I so enjoy the odious mien that the good doctor assumes as I crunch a crackling cockroach or rend the head from a luscious rat, both of which there is an endless supply.

From my hidden perch beneath the stone staircase, I can observe the scene before me. My master's bloodlust for Miss Westenra is palpable. I am certain she will receive an unexpected visit tonight from him. Both the ladies appear to be more than entranced by my master, the ever-gracious host.

Upon their departure, my master summons me. "Renfield," he says, his Eastern European accent apparent. "I vould very much like to indulge myself vith Miss Lucy this evening. Please meet me vhen I return."

"Yes, Master," I reply.

And with that he transforms himself into a large bat. He hovers in the room, waiting for me to the open the massive front entry door and make his egress.

I smile with satisfaction. I am the perfect majordomo.

I will make my return to the asylum after daybreak when my master has fed and returned to his place of repose. My "keepers" at the asylum, aided by my suggestions, will await my return and facilitate my entrance back into my cell with no one the wiser.

And so things continue for several weeks.

Until I discover, while secretly eavesdropping on a conversation between Seward and a newcomer to the sanitarium, a doctor of sorts as well: Professor Abraham Van Helsing.

Seward: "She is quite pale and listless."

Van Helsing: (With a quite thick German accent) "I am afraid that from all that you have told me, I can come to but one conclusion: your Miss Lucy has been put under the control for the vilest of creature's to ever walk the earth... A Vampire!

Seward: "Surely you must be joking, Abraham. That's preposterous! It is only a legend—"

Van Helsing: "A most real fact!" He slaps his hands together for dramatic effect. "The two small bite marks on her neck, the sleepwalking, the paleness, the lassitude... all of the indications are there." He raises his arm again, as if heading off onto battle. (Quite ludicrous, in fact) "We must act at once!"

His melodramatic gestures and truly poor acting would have had him booed from Shakespeare's stage followed by a volley of various overripe vegetables. A pompous ass, decidedly. Yet, a possible danger as well. A veritable vampire hunter. I must plan carefully.

For as it turns out, my master has also indulged himself with Miss Mina, who has since become Mina Harker.

Yes, I must plan carefully...

Next evening it appears that the dear Professor has indeed proceeded with all haste and precluded my own plotting.

Alas and alack, Miss Lucy Westenra is no longer with us. That buffoon, Van Helsing, with Seward in tow, tracked Miss Lucy down, plunged a stake through her heart and removed her most lovely head.

I must see to it that Van Helsing's vampire hunt comes to an abrupt halt. A plan is beginning to form in my mind. Miss Mina's singular psychic connection to my master may prove to be to my benefit. "Oh, what a tangled web we weave..." Walter Scott had that correct, at least.

My master is most displeased with the "murder" of Miss Lucy. And through my eavesdropping at the asylum, I have learned the despicable duo's devious plan. They hope to use Miss Mina's psychic connection to lead her to my master, and in so doing, dispatch him in the same way they did to Miss Lucy.

The stage is set.

The roles are cast.

Now I must give the players their lines and ensure a flawless performance. And a grand guignol finale!

It is dusk, and Van Helsing and Harker, with several

"keepers" from the asylum, have been led by Miss Mina—with my assistance—to our castle and the resting place of my master.

They are in a furor to get to my master before he awakens. They storm through the main entry and begin searching the premises. It is time for my best scene.

At the top of the staircase, I become irrational and begin spouting seeming nonsense, avowing that Count Dracula is good man, etc. Van Helsing tries to push me aside, and in our struggle, I plummet to, what would assuredly be, my death at the bottom of the staircase.

Caring man that he is, Van Helsing cries, "Leave him. He is dead. We have a more urgent matter!" He rushes by my still form, vampire-killer accoutrements flailing. The ass.

The fall, of course, would have killed a normal man, but as we know, I am not.

After a few moments, my bones have mended, and I surreptitiously follow the vampire killers to see the final act played out.

They have discovered the chamber where the coffins are kept and are furiously opening them in their frantic search to find the coffin that contains my master. Van Helsing is screaming about sacraments and holy water. They are to sanctify the earth in the coffins to prevent being used again. A noble gesture. I chuckle from my place of concealment.

I hear a cry and a gasp from Van Helsing and Harker.

They have found him.

"Hurry, Harker. We have not time to waste. You must do it now!" I hear Van Helsing bellow. My contempt for him knows no bounds. I peer around the marble slab where I have been concealing myself and observe Harker raising a wooden stake above his head, then plunging it downward into my master's heart.

"Excellent! Now we must remove the head," Van Helsing yells and proceeds to do exactly that, with a good degree of difficulty, I might add.

"It is done," Van Helsing states, exhaustion sounding with every word. "We must destroy all of the coffins as well. Remove this abhorrent evil."

Mina, who had been standing stolidly still, observing this mayhem, now takes the stage. "Where am I? What has happened? I feel so exhausted." A convincing performance.

Harker rushed to her. "My beloved, it is done. The perfidious demon has been destroyed." Mina collapses against him, and he proceeds to take her away.

Sometime later, Van Helsing and his minions follow.

I smile.

It is, indeed, done.

My power of suggestion that I have honed, lo these many centuries, has come to its ultimate fruition. Not only did I plant the seeds of suggestion in the lovely Miss Mina, but also with Harker and Van Helsing himself.

In my "sessions" with Harker and Van Helsing, while they were studying me, I was implanting all of the various suggestions for the final outcome.

They did, indeed, stake and behead the poor unfortunate in the coffin they were made to think was my master. They looked at one victim and saw another.

Perhaps my finest hour. Mayhap, I should direct theater. An idea to explore.

My master awaited me on the ship I had acquired in Whitby Harbor for our return to Transylvania. There were many other cities we could inhabit. London seemed destined to be the bane of our existence. Perhaps, Paris...

Now without the threat of that insipid Van Helsing, for, you see, my final suggestion to them was that they will slowly forget we ever visited London or even existed. A little trick I learned from my mistress, centuries ago, Erzsebet.

It was 1608, and The King's Men were touring the continent after another outbreak of plague had occurred in London. We had a command performance in Hungary at the Castle of Csejte, nestled in the Little Carpathian Mountains.

Our patron was Countess Erzsebet Bathory, an entrancing creature if ever there was one.

After our performance of *Othello*—my Iago, as always was mesmerizing—and the Countess thought so as well, as she was later that evening to tell me in her private bedchamber.

The Countess Bathory indulged her carnal, and other, desires with me for the four days we were in residence.

And when I left, I was changed. I was no longer a man...

I was a vampire.

I was also in love with Countess Erzsebet as well. But she no longer wanted anything to do with me. I was her pet, her slave, her concubine for as long as she desired, then I was cast off as rubbish. A devastating blow to my ego as well. I begged, pleaded, cajoled to no effect.

She cruelly laughed me off, emasculating me further, telling me I should be grateful that in a moment of frenzied lust, she had forced me to drink from her, as she had been drinking from me.

Her blood had made me immortal.

Albeit, that was all I had learned about existing as a vampire. That, and the fact I could make someone obey me with the hypnotic power of suggestion. The rest I would discover for myself over the ensuing centuries.

Alas, the one thing I did not discover until 250 years hence was that I had impregnated the Countess.

She had a child who would inherit her castle in neigh-
boring Transylvania.

Her son.

My son.

The Count Dracula.

WHAT ONCE WAS FLESH

TIM WAGGONER

"You got some blood on the corner of your mouth," Al said.

An unnaturally long black tongue slithered out of Dylan's mouth to lap away the excess gore. He smacked his lips when he was finished.

"You gotta watch little details like that. That's the sort of thing that'll give you away."

"You telling me someone will see a smear of red on my mouth and think, 'Holy shit! That guy's a vampire!'" Dylan smirked. "I doubt it."

"Human senses may be duller than ours, but they can recognize a predator when they spot one – at least on a subconscious level. People start getting suspicious of you, they'll call the cops. That happens, and you'll have to find new a hunting ground. As it is, we can only stay in the same area a few months. A year tops, if we're careful. Why make life harder on yourself if you don't have to?"

"Yeah, I guess so," Dylan said grudgingly.

The two men sat in the front seat of a red-and-white van with the words *Community EMS* painted on the side. There was nothing to identity *what* community, which was exactly the way Al wanted it. In a town of any decent size, people – even police – didn't look twice at emergency medical vehicles. Not only was it a great cover, it was a damned good lure, too. The blue uniforms Al and Dylan wore put people immediately at ease, and it wasn't uncommon for someone to approach them with some sort of medical emergency and ask for their help. Talk about having your food delivered! And if a cop ever did pull them over, they had a plausible reason for why someone was strapped down to a gurney in the back. *Just transporting a patient, officer. Acute anemia. Real serious.*

Al had parked the van outside a UtiliMart, two rows away from a fluorescent lamppost. He wanted their vehicle to be visible, but not *too* visible. He'd been running the EMS scam for four years now, moving from town to town as necessary, and if there was one thing he'd learned, it was that, as in real estate, success was spelled location, location, location. And an extra-large helping of patience didn't hurt, either – especially when it came to breaking in a new partner.

Dylan was in his late twenties, stocky, with a shaved head, stubbly beard, expanders in his ears, and tattoos over much of his body. He looked like a tough customer, but when it came to vampirism, he was about as green as they came. He'd been turned less than a month ago, not by Al, but by some bitch working the prostitute angle, a scam as old as the Pleistocene. She hadn't stayed with Dylan. Why would she? Most humans didn't turn after they'd been drained, and most vampires had a "feed or die" mentality when it came to any progeny they might unwittingly create. Al had found Dylan working a rest stop in Kentucky, doing his best to subsist on the occasional sips of blood he managed to steal from truckers. He'd been half-starved and half-crazed when Al took him in, and they'd been traveling together ever since while Al showed him the ropes.

The first thing Al had taught the dumbass: It's not just blood they fed on, but blood *and* death. For blood to be truly nourishing, their prey had to die. Not right away, but eventually. There was something about having your teeth buried in the flesh of your prey as they died – being so intimately connected as the life fled their body – that charged the blood in your belly and turned it into fiery liquid more potent than rocket fuel. If your victim didn't die, you might as well be drinking water.

Speaking of victims, they'd had good hunting tonight. They'd picked up a jogger in a suburban neighborhood soon after sunset, and they'd each drank from her, although Al had let Dylan finish her off. He was still hungry, but he didn't feel deprived. He was saving his appetite. The jogger's corpse was in the back, strapped to the gurney, covered by a sheet. When he could, Al liked to wait a bit before disposing of his empties, just in case they turned. But it had been a couple hours since the jogger had died, and she hadn't so much as twitched in all that time. He decided to give it a little longer.

He settled back against his seat and watched the shoppers outside come and go from their cars, much as a lion watches animals move across the Savanna. Not necessarily hungry, but still alert for an opportunity too good to pass up. Al looked to be in his sixties, although he was far older. His skin was sallow, almost jaundiced, and he was thin to the point of being gaunt. He wore his brown hair short, and although he'd sported many hairstyles over the centuries, he liked his current haircut best. It didn't get in the way, and it didn't give prey anything to grab hold of. His eyes were brown, too, although when the hunger was upon him, they appeared jet black. Like now.

Dylan lit a cigarette and took a long drag. He cracked the passenger window and blew the smoke out. Regardless of their habits in life, most vampires didn't smoke. Their heightened senses rendered all forms of tobacco noxious to them. But Dylan was still a child in darkness, his senses nowhere near as sharp as they could be.

"I got a question for you, Al."

"Yeah?"

"A lot of times you talk about us like an announcer in a nature documentary. To hear you tell it, we're apex predators, the very tip-top of the food chain. But we're more than that, aren't we?"

Al frowned. "I'm not sure what you mean."

"Well, we're . . . you know. *Evil*, right?" He grinned, displaying elongated incisors. He hadn't yet learned how to conceal his fangs without concentrated effort.

Up to this point, Al had kept his gaze fixed on the people passing by. Now he turned his head to look at Dylan. "What exactly do you mean by evil?"

His smile widened too far, and tiny fissures opened at the corners of his mouth. Clear fluid beaded forth from the wounds, but Dylan seemed unaware of them. Vampires were so strong they could easily injure themselves, but since they were so resistant to pain, they often didn't realize it. *Good thing we heal so fast,* Al thought. And as if the thought gave birth to reality, the fissures in Dylan's mouth closed, though the beads of liquid remained.

"Evil," Dylan repeated. "Princes of Darkness, Lords of the Night, that kind of thing."

Al's smile was smaller and more controlled than Dylan's. "So melodramatic. Did you read too many comics as a child?

Yes, we are creatures of evil, for lack of a better word. It's why we shun daylight, avert our gazes from holy objects of all sorts, and why our flesh burns if it comes in contact with them. And of course, it's why we must feed as we do. But all of these qualities are symptoms of our true condition. We have no souls."

From the bemused look on Dylan's face, Al knew he wasn't following.

"Human beings are born with souls. It's what sets them apart from all other creatures on Earth. When a human becomes a vampire, the physical body reanimates, but the soul is no longer present. This is why our kind can kill without hesitation or remorse. No soul, no conscience. It's a very useful adaptation. You can't be an effective predator if you're burdened by a conscience."

Dylan took another drag on his cigarette and stared out the window for several moments before speaking again.

"So where does it go? The soul, I mean."

Despite his long years of practiced control, Al had to fight to keep from grinning so wide that he ripped his own cheeks wide open. Dylan had finally asked The Question, the one every vampire came to eventually. And he had asked it at precisely the right time.

"Some self-styled experts in the occult believe that a vampire's soul is damned to Hell until its body is destroyed, thereby freeing the spirit to enter Heaven. But this is nothing more than a fairy tale concocted by humans. The truth is far more interesting. Do you really want to know where your soul is now?"

"Yeah."

Al turned and pointed at a man walking past their van. He wore a faded army jacket, old jeans, and running shoes on the verge of falling apart. His head was shaved, his body tattooed, and the holes in his earlobes were held open by large metal rings.

"It's right there."

"This is so freaky!" Dylan said.

The two vampires stood in an aisle in Utilimart's electronics department. The other Dylan was less than thirty feet away from them, examining a cell phone display with a vacant, almost lost expression on his face, as if he wasn't quite sure what he was doing here.

"Keep your voice down," Al hissed. "As long as you stay close to me, I can use my powers to conceal your presence from him, but he isn't deaf. Once you attract his attention, I won't be able to hide you again."

Dylan whispered this time. "You say that's my soul, but he looks solid enough. Is he some kind of ghost? If I walked over and tried to poke him, would my finger pass through his body?"

"He would feel like flesh and bone to you, but I wouldn't advise getting that close. He might not look dangerous, but he's the closest thing to a natural predator that our kind has. Or should I say, that *you* have."

"I don't get it."

The other Dylan turned away from the cell phones and headed to the aisle where the DVD's were kept. Al and the real Dylan followed at a discrete distance. The other Dylan paused before the comedies as if he might browse them, but he just stared at the titles with the same blank expression on his face.

"If you think of vampirism as a spiritual disease, then beings like him are antibodies," Al said. "When a new vampire is created, the mortal soul is cast out of its body and remains earthbound. Eventually, the soul – the Animus – is compelled to seek out the corrupt creature that stole its body and attempt to destroy it. It never tires, and it will not stop until its mission is complete . . . or until it is neutralized."

"What's the big deal?" Dylan said. "He doesn't look so tough. I'll just walk over and tear his head off, and we'll call it a night." He took a step toward his other self, but Al grabbed hold of his arm and stopped him.

"Don't be fooled by his appearance. He's just as strong and resistant to damage as we are – and he has none of our weaknesses."

Dylan looked skeptical. "If you say so. But even if it's true, so what? There are two of us and one of him. All we have to do is tag team him."

"It's not that simple. Killing one's own soul is the final act of evil that completes our transformation. Once you do it, you'll be truly immortal. Otherwise, even though you are a vampire, you will age and die just as any mortal. But *you* have to do it. Your Animus can only perish at your hands. No one else's."

The other Dylan moved on from comedies and was now standing in the children's section. Al and the real Dylan could still see him, so they stayed where they were.

"Did you kill your soul?" Dylan asked.

"Yes. And it was the toughest battle I've ever been in. I'd rather face a dozen of our kind in combat than a single Animus."

Dylan continued looking at his other self for a few moments, and when next he spoke, he sounded overly nonchalant, as if he were scared and working hard not to show it. "So . . . what do I do?"

Before Al could respond, the other Dylan's head snapped up and turned in their direction. His eyes narrowed, as if he were trying to see them but had trouble focusing his vision. Al grabbed hold of Dylan's arm again so they would be in physical contact, the better to extend his glamour over the other vampire.

"Don't move," he breathed.

They stood absolutely motionless in the way that only the dead can do, and after a few moments, Dylan's Animus looked away and wandered off to another section of the store.

Still keeping hold of Dylan's arm, Al led him toward the exit.

"Come on. We have work to do."

"Why didn't you warn me about him before?" Dylan asked. He tossed another shovelful of earth out of the hole he'd been digging, hurling it with such strength that it flew a dozen yards away to join the rest of the soil strewn there. The hole – a small pit by this point, really – was square, four feet deep and six feet across. Dylan stood inside, doing the excavating, while Al remained topside, supervising.

Dylan sounded pissed, and Al supposed he couldn't blame him.

"You're not the first vampire I've mentored. Ever heard the phrase 'Seeing is believing'? Why do you think we've spent so much time hanging out in parking lots the last couple weeks? I've been waiting for your Animus to track you down so I could show it to you – and I wanted to give you more time to grow stronger, so you'd have a better chance of defeating it."

"The least you could do is get in here and help me dig," Dylan said, sounding like a sulky child.

"I told you, I need to keep watch. We don't want your Animus sneaking up on us, and since I'm so much older than you, my senses are stronger. I'll know when it's within half a mile of here."

The two vampires were in a field beneath a clear night sky. A crescent sliver of a moon hung overhead, nestled in an ebony expanse dotted with glittering stars. Nights like tonight, it was good to be undead, Al thought. An abandoned farmhouse and barn sat on the property, two black shapes silhouetted against the horizon. The Community EMS van was parked inside the empty barn, lights off, of course.

Dylan removed a couple more shovelfuls of dirt before speaking again.

"I don't see how this is going to work. You said my Animus is just as tough as we are. How is falling into a pit going to hurt it? And really, do you think it's stupid enough to fall for a trick like this?"

"It's not intelligent, per se. As I said earlier, it's like an antibody. It doesn't think; it just acts and reacts. I stopped cloaking your presence over an hour ago, so your Animus is undoubtedly on your trail and headed this way. Once it sees you, it'll make a beeline straight for you, and as long as you're standing on the other side of the pit, it'll tumble right in. Hell, by that point, it'll be so excited that we probably don't even need to cover the pit, but we'll put some trees branches over it and lay some sod on top, just to be sure. When you finish digging the pit, we'll put sharpened stakes in the bottom. They won't kill the Animus. It's not a vampire. But they will hold it in place long enough for you to jump in and sink your fangs into its neck. The only thing that can kill your Animus is the bite from a vampire. But not just any vampire: you."

Dylan flung another shovelful of dirt out of the pit, and then looked up at Al, a skeptical expression on his face.

"Are you sure about this?"

Al smiled. "Have I steered you wrong yet?"

"It's close," Al said.

He stood next to Dylan at the edge of the pit. They'd waited like this for several hours, during which Dylan had run through all of his cigarettes. The stink of tobacco hung heavy in the air, but Al didn't complain. He had been in Dylan's shoes once, and he understood how nervous the younger vampire was. It was a hell of a thing, finding yourself transformed into a bad-ass monster, only to discover that there was something out there just as dangerous as you whose only purpose was to take you out.

"I think I can hear him," Dylan said softly.

Al had been able to hear the Animus approaching for the last ten minutes, its footsteps steady and regular, machine-precise. If he was right, the thing was just about close enough to –

The pace of its footfalls suddenly picked up, shoes pounding the earth, waist-high grass rustling as it raced toward them.

"It's coming," Al said. "Remember what I told you. Once it falls into the pit, strike fast and kill it quick. You won't get a second chance."

Before Dylan could say anything, he moved several

yards back from the pit. This was the younger vampire's battle, and he had to fight it alone.

Dylan instinctively assumed the classic vampire defensive position. He crouched, knees bent, hands outstretched, fingernails lengthening into talons. And although his back was turned, Al knew his canines extended into sabers that hung past his chin, and his jaw unhinged so he could take the biggest bite possible out of his opponent.

Good lad, he thought.

Dylan's Animus made no sound as it came for him. Al had always found their silence to be one of the eeriest things about Animi, but far worse was the expression on their faces when they attacked. They didn't look angry or excited. They weren't filled with rage or possessed by bloodlust. They appeared totally at peace, smiling, arms lifted as if they wanted to embrace their other selves instead of annihilate them. Seeing that expression was the only time Al regretted being a vampire, and even though this wasn't his Animus, he experienced a split second wherein he wished he hadn't vanquished his own soul. What would it be like to feel such peace? To be truly at rest? But he quickly shoved such thoughts aside. They were part of the Animus' attack, a psychic assault designed to make their victims hesitate at the crucial moment. He hoped Dylan would be able to resist it.

Dylan's stance relaxed somewhat as the Animus came toward him, and if it hadn't been for the pit, Al feared the soul creature would've succeeded in claiming him. But true to its nature, the Animus ran straight toward Dylan without paying any attention to its surroundings, and when its foot came down on the branches covering the pit, it fell in face-first. It made no noise as the stakes pierced its flesh, other than letting out a slight outrush of air from its lungs.

"Now!" Al shouted.

Dylan hesitated a split second, and then leaped into the pit. An instant later, Al heard the sound of his saber teeth latching onto the Animus. This was followed by loud sucking noises, accompanied by ecstatic moans. Al waited a moment longer, and then strolled to the edge of the pit.

Dylan was hunched over his Animus, his mouth buried deep in his other's self's neck. He'd bitten into its flesh with such savagery that the Animus' head had almost been severed, but what spilled out of the wound wasn't blood. It was a thick golden liquid that looked something like luminescent honey. As Dylan drank, his body spasmed repeatedly, as if he were caught in the throes of an intense orgasm.

"Feels good, doesn't it?" Al said. "If human blood is like wine to us, then the ichor that flows from the veins of an Animus is like a combination of every drug that ever existed. Ambrosia of the gods. There's only one thing as good: when that ambrosia has been filtered through the body of another vampire."

Al jumped into the pit, grabbed hold of his protégé by the shoulders, and sank his own saber teeth into his throat. Dylan couldn't stop draining his Animus. Once the process had begun, it had to be finished. A tidbit of information that Al had failed to pass along to his student. So as Dylan filled his belly, Al in turn filled his. And when it was all over, the Animus was dead, and so was Dylan.

Al, sated, crawled forth from the pit. His limbs were heavy, and he felt so lethargic, he could barely move. He glanced at the sky and saw it was a shade lighter in the east. Dawn was near. He needed to bury Dylan and the Animus before he could rest, though. Good thing the pit doubled as a ready-made grave.

He picked up the shovel and got to it.

He was inside the EMS vehicle—the barn door closed – before the first rays of sunlight pinked the horizon. He was so weary that it took a major effort of will to keep his eyes open as he climbed into the back of the van. He'd intended to lie down on the gurney, but he swore when he saw the body of the jogger was still strapped there. He'd forgotten all about her. He should've tossed her into the grave with Dylan and the Animus. Oh, well. Too late now. He'd take care of it after sundown.

He started to unbuckle the corpse, intending to dump it onto the floor so he could lie down, when it suddenly took in a gasping breath and opened its eyes.

"Where am I?" the woman said. "What happened?"

Al smiled when he saw her fangs.

"Don't worry. Everything's okay. I'll explain later, but right now you have to sleep. All right?"

She looked at him for a moment, but the daylight torpor was already taking hold of her. She nodded once, closed her eyes, relaxed and fell still.

Al let her keep the gurney. The floor would be fine today. As full as he was, he would sleep well, regardless, and tonight, once the two of them had awakened, he would begin training his new protégé, the latest of many he'd had over the long years. He settled onto the floor and closed his eyes.

Life was good.

THE MUMMY

LEAH SNOW

If you had asked an infinite number of Sam Kennedys when he was younger, maybe in elementary school, what he wanted to do when he grew up, none of them, out of all the countless universe-spanning Sam Kennedys, would have selected running a self-storage center with his stepmother.

Elementary school Sam Kennedy would have said he wanted to be a pro baseball player and in high school, maybe a lawyer or movie producer. But after two years at Northern Arizona University, where he acquitted himself with a 1.25 GPA, Sam realized that higher education wasn't for him. He didn't want to work for some big corporation. He was a man of the people and wasn't meant to be a slave to The Man.

He was more of the entrepreneurial type, so he and his friend Travis started a mobile car detailing company in Flagstaff. It didn't get as hot in Flagstaff as it did in most of Arizona, but getting up early, buffing and vacuuming, and dealing with tight-fisted customers all day took its toll. They went from six cars a day to three, then one, then none. Less than six months after they started, Travis moved back in with his parents in Tucson and Sam had no desire to run the business on his own. He sold the detailing equipment and, like Travis, moved back home.

Sam's father, at least, had understood. "College isn't for everyone," he said to Sam two nights after Sam's ignoble return from Flagstaff and college, after his step-mother Maxine had gone to bed. He and his father sat in lawn chairs on the rear patio of their apartment beneath the immense Arizona sky, nursing beers. "You tried to start your own business. That's something. How many people can say that?"

Sam took a long drink from his beer. "I just don't know what I want to do with my life. What my purpose is."

"You're still young," Dad said. "You have plenty of time to figure it out."

Sam grunted in response, and Dad leaned over and put a hand on Sam's shoulder. When Sam reached up to cover it with his own hand, Dad pulled away. But that was okay. Dad was Dad. He kept his emotions close. The hand on the shoulder was like a hug from most dads. Maxine was more than emotional enough for the two of them, he had once whispered to Sam and his sister during one of his step-mom's many extended crying sessions.

Even before his ill-fated attempt at entrepreneurship, his father had suggested on more than one occasion that Sam should work with him at U-Store-It Self Storage, his storage center in Kingman, Arizona. Sam had always declined. He didn't know what he wanted to do with his life, but he knew it wasn't working a dead end job at a storage center.

Yet that's where he found himself, three months after his father's death, as he jerked awake to the sound of his cell phone vibrating and buzzing on the nightstand. He reached out for the offending piece of glass and plastic, finally touching it with clumsy fingers, and sent it tumbling to the floor.

"Shit," he muttered, and slid over to the edge of the bed. He felt around for the phone as it continued to ring and scooped it, opened one eye, thumbed the answer button and held it to his ear.

"Yeah," he said, or tried to say. It was more of a croak. He had a massive hangover and it hurt to breathe, let alone speak. His lips felt as if they were glued together. His head was stuffed with angry bees.

"Turn that down!" came a voice through the wall. His step-mom was Maxine in the next room.

"Hey, sorry to wake you," said Jackson, the caretaker, gofer, security man, etc. at the storage center. "We have a problem over here in Building A."

"A problem," Sam said. "Uh... um..."

"... in Building A," Jackson finished for him.

Sam opened his other eye and squinted at his phone. 6:12 am. Shit. He had gotten in at about three. "Can't it wait?" he said.

There was a moment of hesitation, and Sam was sure Jackson was going to tell him that yes, it could in fact wait, and he'd see Sam in about ten hours. But what Jackson said was, "It's pretty important. We should handle it as soon as we can."

The metal door to Building A slammed shut, the sound echoing through the cavernous storage building. Jackson looked up as Sam strode toward him, clad in pajama pants and a Kiss t-shirt. His flip-flops made angry slapping sounds on the concrete floor.

"So, what's the problem?" Sam said, stifling a yawn. "What couldn't wait until we open?"

"Something weird. I didn't know what to do," Jackson said. He was wide awake, which only made Sam's hangover worse. At least the bees had settled down.

"'Didn't know what to do?'" Sam said, a little more nasty than necessary. "You had to wake me up? You couldn't figure it out yourself?"

"Not this," Jackson said. "This can't wait."

"Well, you woke up Maxine too, so it better be important."

Jackson nodded. "It's important, all right."

Jackson grabbed the handle at the bottom of the shuttered metal door and heaved it up. The rollers rocked and rumbled, revealing an almost empty ten by ten storage unit. Almost empty.

Sam took a step forward, glanced inside, and then backed up quickly, nearly bumping into Jackson. "Holy shit," he said. "Is that a body?"

"Looks like it," Jackson said. "That's why I called you."

Sam leaned in for another look. In most of the nicer, modern storage units, each unit had its own light switch. But "U-Store-It Self Storage" was neither nice nor modern, so the only light available were the bulbs mounted on the corridor ceiling every ten feet or so. He had promised himself, after his father died and he had taken it over—well, he and his stepmother—that one of the first things he was going to do was to put lights in the units. But three months later, he hadn't done much more than organize the crap on top of his desk.

Sam turned on the flashlight on his phone. He aimed it into the storage unit. In the center of the empty space, lying on its side in the fetal position, was the mummified body of either a small adult or a child. Thick strands of brown twine were wrapped around the entirety of its body, keeping its knees pulled up tight to its chest and over its folded arms. It wasn't wrapped all in strips of cloth like the mummies in the movies. It wore the ragged remains of a primitive shirt and pants. But it was a mummy all right. It was one hundred percent mummified.

"Why would someone do this?" Sam asked. He didn't need this. He needed coffee.

Jackson had no response.

Sam angled his light from side to side. More twine was stretched along both the left and right metal walls. Hanging from each length of twine were dozens of knotted strings of different lengths. This was repeated from the top of each wall to the floor, every two feet or so, resulting in what had to be hundreds of dangling strings.

Colorful stones and several small cloth-wrapped objects formed a rough semicircle around the body.

"What the fuck is all that?" Sam said.

Again, Jackson didn't reply. Sam turned his light off and stepped into the hallway.

"Was this unit in default?" Sam said. It seemed like all he was doing was asking questions. And Jackson had no answers. Sam's phone buzzed. He glanced down at it. Maxine. He swore softly and put the phone to his ear.

"Hey, Maxine," he said, closed his eyes, and listened. "Yeah, I know, and I'm sorry about that. Uh huh... Uh huh... Well, I thought I was being quiet. I know. I know. I will. So, you'll never guess—" He listened again, then hung his head. "Was that today? One o'clock? Sure, sure, I'll be re—" He stopped, said, "Hello?" then held his phone away from his ear and looked at it. He slid his phone back in his pocket.

Jackson held out a manila folder. "This is all the paper-work I could find, but it's really weird. Just this."

Sam took the folder. He removed a single sheet of paper and moved beneath the bulb to read.

Jackson glanced over at him, but his eyes were drawn back to the figure on the bare concrete floor. He wasn't sure, but it appeared to be clutching something close to its chest. He moved a little closer to better examine it.

"This is crazy," Sam flipped the paper over and read it again. "Someone, with really shitty handwriting by the way, paid my dad sixteen thousand dollars in cash about... twenty two years ago..." He read from the paper, "...to keep residence in storage unit A24..." he glanced up, confirming that this was indeed storage unit A24, and then back to the paper. "...in perpetuity. What does that even mean? It's handwritten! How is this even legal?" He turned to Jackson and waved the paper at him. "Did you know anything about this?"

Jackson, bent at the waist with his hands on his knees, was staring at the body

"Jackson," said Sam. "Did my dad ever say anything about this unit?"

Without turning, Jackson said, "I think I asked him about it once, and he told me not to worry about it."

"So, we have no way of knowing who rented this unit?"

Jackson stood up and shook his head and pointed at the bottom of the page that Sam held. "Not unless you can read that signature on the contract."

"This is unbelievable." Sam shook his head in disbelief. Shaking was a mistake. It woke the bees.

Sam said, "Tell me again what happened."

Jackson nodded. "After the first no payment, policy is that we call the renter. Only this one..." He gestured to the folder. "... doesn't have a phone number or an address. So I cut the lock off. And I rolled the door up and opened the unit and saw..." He nodded at the corpse. "That, and I called you."

Sam looked over the single sheet of paper again. "There's no way of getting in touch with the owners?" He asked the questions out loud, but he was talking to himself. Not that it mattered, because Jackson wasn't listening.

Jackson tossed the padlock nervously from hand to hand. He tried to look at Sam, but he couldn't. His eyes were drawn not so much to the shape on the floor, but at what it looked to be clutching to its chest. He could glimpse something between its arms. Was that wood? "What do you think it's holding?"

Sam hadn't really noticed. The fact that there was a dead body in a storage unit in a facility he now owned—with his step-mom, technically, but who cared—was the problem. He looked more closely and saw that the body did in fact have something clutched tightly to its chest.

"I think it's a box," Jackson said, as if reading his mind. "You want me to get it?" His voice was lowered, almost as if he didn't want the mummy to hear what he was saying. Sam didn't like the look in Jackon's eyes. Normally his eyes were cloudy, the blue faded away like sun bleached paint, but now, now they were bright. Jackson was excited.

But he had to admit, hungover or not, he was kind of curious. Besides, whatever it was now belonged to them.

"Yeah. Sure. Knock yourself out."

As Jackson stepped into the storage unit, Sam stared at the still form on the floor. Its legs were drawn up to the chest, covering up the folded arms. The face, what was left of it, was smooth and taut, the eyes slitted and the nose a dark hole. The lips had pulled back into a grotesque smile, revealing a mouthful of large yellowed teeth.

Would he be liable for it? It was his property, sure, but how was he supposed to know what some sicko kept in their storage unit? It had probably sat here for years. He had only been running the place for three months. What would it do for business if this got out? And what would Maxine say?

He watched as Jackson struggled to pull the mummy's arms away from its chest. After he took over the storage lot, he kept Jackson on because he felt sorry for him. Jackson was pretty old, but he was a hard worker. He lived in a motorhome parked at the back of the lot.

Sometimes he smelled like booze, but he did his job. Jackson was okay. His step-mom had wanted to fire him, saying they didn't need him, but Sam had argued that there was no one who else would work 24-7 for basically room and board. He was a handyman, gofer, and security guard all in one. And best of all, Sam paid him in cash so his salary didn't show up on the books. That had shut her down, at least. Nothing could shut her *up*.

He watched Jackson strain at the cords binding the body, but despite their age, they were still strong. He was pulling the body off the floor, moving it around, and it made Sam a little nauseous. Finally, Jackson dropped the body and, without looking up, said "I'm going to use my knife." He reached down and pulled a folding knife from his pocket. He opened the knife expertly, with just his thumb, and began sawing at the cords. He grunted with effort.

"They're tougher than they look," he said. But eventually, a strand fell to the floor. Then another. A breeze brushed through Sam's hair and he shivered. He glanced up at the ventilation system. Just the air turning on. No need to get all excited.

Jackson set the knife down and tore some of the last strands free, then leaned in and bent the arms back—which creeped Sam out—pulling them away from the body. He looked like he was wrestling with it, and for a brief second Sam thought... but then Jackson dropped the body and came away holding a dark object.

"What is it?" Sam said.

Jackson stood at the entrance to unit A24 and looked down at what he held in his hands. As Sam approached, Jackson looked up and took a step back.

"Dude," Sam said. "Let me see it." He held out his hands.

Reluctantly, like a dog being forced to drop a favorite toy, Jackson handed Sam a dark wooden box. He stepped away from Sam, but his eyes never left the box. Sam examined the box, noting how heavy it was for its size. It was about as big as a thick hardcover book. The top was covered not with writing, but with tiny images and shapes etched into the wood, crosses and half circles, and every so often a human figure or head. He traced one of the shapes with a finger. What did they say? Was it Egyptian? It looked a lot like those little picture letters that the Egyptians used. He tried to open it, but it was locked. He turned it and saw that there was a tiny keyhole that would require, obviously, a tiny key.

"- bust it open?"

Startled, Sam looked up. Jackson stood beside him, holding a screwdriver.

Sam shook his head. "Isn't there a key? Maybe in the folder or..." he looked down at the mummy, now splayed out on its back, where Jackson had dumped it. He saw a tiny key dangling from a chain around its neck. He pointed. "There's the key."

Jackson scrambled over to the mummy and knelt beside

it and pulled at the chain. The head sagged as he lifted the body off the floor.

"Be careful, "Sam said. "You're going to... hurt it." It was out before he realized how stupid he sounded.

Jackson rolled the mummy onto its side and unfastened a clasp. He handed the key to Sam. It was tiny and Sam had to hold it using the tips of his fingers. He dropped it, and then as he bent to pick it up, he accidentally kicked it back into the storage space. It clattered beside the mummy, flat on its back, its empty eyes staring up at the ceiling. Sam paused and Jackson swooped to pick the key up.

"You want me to try?" Jackson said.

Sam snatched the key from him. "No, I can do it." He carefully inserted the key in the lock, but it wouldn't turn.

"You might have to force it," Jackson said. "It's pretty old."

"I know what I have to do," Sam said. "I have to force it." He held the tiny key as tightly as he could and twisted. Something gave, and he twisted harder. There was a sharp "ping" and the lock opened. He lifted the lid of the box, aware of Jackson crowding him.

The light bulb in the ceiling above them flickered in its wire cage. Neither one of them noticed. They were staring into the chest.

"Holy..." Jackson said

"...shit," Sam finished.

The chest was filled with gleaming gold coins, small carved figurines, golden bracelets, rings, and dozens of bright green gemstones.

Jackson dropped his knife, which clattered on the floor at his feet. He didn't seem to notice. He only had eyes for the contents of the box. He reached a long fingered hand in and touched one of the luminescent green stones. "Are those emeralds?" he said.

Sam pulled the box away, shifting the contents and sending several gems and coins flying. One of them bounced off the wall and rolled across the floor.

"What the hell are you doing?" Sam closed the box and knelt to pick up the spilled loot. "Keep your goddamn hands out of that! It doesn't belong to you."

"What'd I do?" Jackson said. He managed to look offended. "I just wanted to look at it..."

Sam scanned the floor to make sure he had picked up all the gems and coins then turned on Jackson. "Keep your hands to yourself."

"What's the big deal?" Jackson said. "Look at it all. Nobody would miss it if I took one or two."

"It doesn't belong to you," Sam said. He opened the box with one hand, and with the other he dropped the coins back in the box. He closed the lid.

"So, what, then?" Jackson said, his voice getting louder. He moved forward. "I suppose it belongs to you and your mother, is that it? After all I did for your father, you can't even share some of this with me? Do you even know how much I do around here? While you and that fucking lazy bitch sit on your fat asses all day?"" Jackson said. He felt something under his foot and glanced down, realizing he had stepped on a coin.

Now Sam was angry. Tired and hungover, but angry. This was too much. Nobody accused him of having a fat ass. And Maxine was *not* his mother.

"Listen, you piece of shit," Sam said, poking Jackson in the chest. "This is our place. We own it. You don't like it, you can get the hell out."

"Oh, you'd like that, wouldn't you?" Jackson said, trying

to keep from glancing down. "And then what? Who's going to do all the... all the..." He froze, staring at Sam, his face turning red and his eyes bulging.

Jackson started to say something else, but all that came out was, "Gurp..." A trickle of blood ran down his chin. His Adam's apple began to grow, extending outward.

Sam watched, transfixed, forgetting about the treasure he held in his arms. He was afraid Jackson was having a heart attack. Could this day get any worse?

It could. Jackson's Adam's apple exploded in a burst of red. Sam gasped, instinctively raising his hands to shield his face from the spray of blood.

Jackson dropped to his knees and coughed out a mouthful of blood, gurgled, and pitched forward. His head hit the floor with a loud thunk, like a wooden bat connecting with a baseball. The hilt of a knife protruding from the back of his neck.

Crimson pooled around his head and neck. Sam backed away, sliding through the blood. His face was a mask of terror, his hangover forgotten.

Standing on the other side of Jackson's prone form was the dead body from the storage unit.

Sam froze, face to face with the mummy—a zombie? But weren't mummies just zombies wrapped in rags? It stared back at him with its sunken, empty eye sockets, but deep within the sockets, a sickly green light burned. It gnashed its cracked, grinning teeth and the spell broke.

Sam backed away, sliding on the blood and losing one flipflop, until he butted up against the sliding door of the unit across the way.

The mummy bent, moving in stiff, quick jerks, and grasped the hilt of the knife. It pulled at the knife, but Jackson's head moved with it, and it only succeeded in bending his neck back. His eyes stared, his mouth gaped, and a thick line of blood and saliva trailed from his lower lip. The mummy tugged on the knife, then shook it back and forth, which only made Jackon's head flip from side to side and spatter droplets of blood on the floor and walls.

The mummy looked over at Sam as if saying, "Are you seeing this?", then knelt and placed a foot on Jackson's head and held it down. It pulled the knife free and knelt to pick up the small chest.

Sam continued to slide his back along the metal door, moving away from the mummy while trying to not look like he was doing so. No sudden movements. His back scraped against a padlock, and he grimaced and arched his lower back as he moved, staying as close to the wall as he could.

The mummy pushed one of Jackson's legs to the side and picked up something small and glittering- a coin. It opened the box and dropped the coin inside, then snapped the lid shut.

Sam risked a glance to his left. The outside door was only about twenty feet away, but he wasn't sure he could make it before—the mummy turned its head and held him with its gaze.

Sam froze. *This is it*, he thought. *I am going to die.*

The mummy watched him for a moment longer as Sam pushed himself into the concrete wall behind him. But then a miracle—a miracle! The mummy turned away and, grabbing Jackson by a leg, dragged him into the unit, leaving a trail of blood on that hard concrete floor.

Sam continued toward the exit door, still keeping to the wall, moving slowly. He stared down at his feet, one bare, the other flip-flopped, when there was a booming crash. Sam let out a shriek and spilled to the floor, gasping and sobbing. His bladder let loose. He turned back, expecting to see that horrible grinning thing coming for him, but froze, a scream stuck in his throat. The rolling unit door had been pulled down. The corridor was empty. Warm urine dripped down his thighs.

Whimpering, Sam scrambled to his feet, losing his remaining flip flop in the effort. He crawled the last few feet to the exit door, banged it open, and slid outside. The door clanged shut behind him. He leaned his back against it, whimpering, and slumped to the ground.

"Oh fuck, oh fuck, oh fuck," he whispered.

What was he supposed to do?

His phone vibrated in his pocket, and he reached in and picked it up with two fingers. It was wet. He sniffed it and grimaced. Pee. Was that his? He found a spot on his shirt that wasn't blood spattered and wiped his phone on it.

He looked at the screen, sighed, and put it to his ear.

"Hey, Maxine," he said. Then listened. And listened. She was on a roll. He was irresponsible, she was worried, she never should have let him take over running the place, he was too young, he didn't care about her nerves, and so on.

"Look, I'm gonna have to call you back," he said, and hit the button to hang up. He stood and thought about opening the door and peeking in but decided against it. He'd go over to the office to think this over.

Ten minutes later, Sam's pulse had slowed to its normal rhythm. He had changed his shirt to a promotional U-Store-It Self Storage tee shirt over his damp PJ pants. His feet were still bare. Jackson kept a little desk in the back of the office, and Sam had dug into his bottom drawer and pulled out a bottle of cheap vodka. He'd poured himself a slug, using one of the Garfield coffee mugs Maxine kept beside the coffee machine. The vodka helped. His thoughts were clearer now.

He booted up a computer and pulled up the security camera feed. He clicked around until he found the camera view which overlooked the units in Building A. The live image popped up in fuzzy black and white. The system was old. He turned the brightness up. The corridor was still and empty. Using the keyboard, he rewound it. He wanted to see exactly what the fuck happened. Or try to. He really wasn't sure how to do it. Maxine usually handled the camera. She loved clicking from camera to camera, watching people load and unload stuff into their units, making comments on what they wore and how cheap their furniture looked and what she imagined they had in their boxes.

He hit the pause button. He watched the screen as Jackson carried the chest into the center of the corridor. Sam fast forwarded a little. They were facing each other now, arms waving. He felt a stab of guilt for the way he shouted at Jackson. But he had been right. The box *was* his. He owned this place. And by law, whatever was in that unit now belonged to him. *Whatever was in that unit...* the phrase chilled him. There was a fucking walking, murderous corpse in that unit. He shook his head, hit the "play" button.

The grainy black and white figures continued arguing, and then—the screen went dark.

"Shit!" Sam pushed the play button again. The time stamp was running, counting off the seconds, but the screen was black. He whacked the side of the monitor, but nothing changed. Black screen. He checked to make sure the cables were plugged in. He watched as the time stamp in the corner of the dark screen continued to count down until an image popped up on the screen. The corridor. The unit. No Jackson. No Sam. No mummy, if that's what it even was.

Only one thing had changed. Now there were some dark stains on the floor.

Sam hit the rewind button, but the same thing happened. Right before the mummy showed up, the screen went dark. No sign of the mummy or Jackson's dead body.

Sam leaned back in the chair, staring at the screen and chewing a fingernail.

What the fuck was he supposed to do now?

He couldn't tell his step-mom. She'd somehow blame it on him. She said, just last week, "If you had finished college, you would have a real job and we could have sold this piece of shit and we could be living in a house like your sister."

It wasn't his fault he didn't finish college. Those professors taught what they wanted, not what *he* wanted. He told himself that if his father hadn't died, he would go back and finish… once he figured out what he wanted to do.

If Maxine found out what had happened to Jackson, she would call the cops first thing, mummy or no mummy. He couldn't have that. Cops would show up, seal off the unit with that yellow tape, take the mummy and the little box and mark it "Exhibit A" or something like that. He'd never see it again.

And let's not forget that Jackson was dead, and what would Sam tell them, that the mummy had stood up and stuck a knife in Jackson's neck? How would that go over? The last recording on the security system was him and Jackson arguing. Case closed, as far as the cops were concerned.

He'd have to get rid of the evidence. The mummy and Jackson and all that shit hanging from the walls in the unit and, of course, the security recording. The recording would be easy… but what if the cops wanted to see it? If only that one part was missing, wouldn't that look suspicious?

"Fuck!" Sam slammed his fist down on the desk, nearly toppling the vodka bottle. Why couldn't things ever be easy? He'd have to erase the entire tape and just claim there was some sort of glitch. But Maxine watched the tape every day. She'd know he was lying.

"Fuck! Fuck! Fuck!" This time the vodka bottle did fall over, but Sam stopped it before it hit the floor. He set it back in the drawer and slid it shut. He'd have to erase the whole tape. That was the only way. And somehow keep her from noticing. Or making a fuss.

Jackson's body was another story. That would take time. He glanced up at the clock. It was nearly eight. They opened at nine. If he had to, he would leave the "closed" sign up out front until he figured this out. If people wanted to get into their units, they would have to wait. Fuck 'em. It was as simple as that. He reached for the mug, which still had some vodka in it, and finished it.

Sam opened the door to Building A and stuck his head in and peered down the hallway. All was still.

"Hello?" he said. He hoped to God nobody answered. In any case, there wasn't one, so he stepped into the building. He had a bucket filled with hot soapy water, and he rolled it over the red puddle and began mopping it up. He picked up his discarded flip flops and put them back on. The blood was still fresh, so it didn't take long. He brought some rags which he used to wipe down the roll down door across from A24. As he finished and was all set to wheel the bucket, now filled with a dark pink water, out the door, he saw a dark line of blood along the bottom of the A24's door. That wouldn't do. He pushed the mop against the bottom of the door and slid it back and forth, but he couldn't get it all. Even with the door closed and locked, someone was bound to notice. And since he wouldn't be able to get the mop head all the way beneath the door, he saw only one solution, which he didn't like. He'd have to raise the door.

"Shit," he said.

But if Sam was being honest with himself, he would admit there was another reason he wanted to open the unit.

He reached out to the door and gave three quick taps, then backed away.

He tilted his head, listening. Nothing.

He approached the door and slid it up a few inches, then scooted away, ready to ditch his flip flops and run.

Nothing happened.

He got on his hands and knees, and using his phone flashlight, put his head down along the floor and shone his light through the narrow opening. The mummy lay on the floor where it was before, once again clutching the dark wooden box to its chest. But now he had company. Jackson's corpse was beside the mummy. His dead eyes stared at the ceiling. Sam raised the door several inches. The mummy didn't move. It just stayed there. Dead.

Sam slid the door higher. The mummy didn't move. He raised the door all the way, his eyes never leaving the still form. Nothing.

He took the mop and cleaned up the remaining blood, extending the mop as close to Jackson as he could, removing the slick dark trail that led to his body. His eyes kept moving from the mummy to the wooden chest. He reached out the mop and nudged the mummy. It didn't react. Emboldened, he touched the mop handle against the chest. Still no movement. Leaning closer, he wedged the mop handle against the lid of the chest and levered it so that the lid opened just an inch or so...

The mummy's eyes blazed green and it turned its head to look at him. And even worse, Jackson's body also jerked, and his mouth gaped open in a soundless scream as he too raised his head and glared at Sam.

Sam was halfway down the corridor before the mop handle hit the floor.

He stood by the exit door, waiting. When nothing followed him, he waited five more minutes. Finally, he ventured back and peeked inside the unit. The mop was on the floor where he had left it. The mummy was dead again. Jackson was flat on his back.

Sam yanked the mop out of the unit and closed the door. This time he shot the bolt, locking it from the outside.

———

He sat at his desk, staring at the computer monitor. The black and white image of the unit might as well have been a photograph. Nothing moved. Nothing changed. Just like the mummy. And Jackson. They hadn't moved... until he had touched the wooden box. The box set them off.

His phone buzzed, and without looking away from the monitor he slid the answer button.

Thirty seconds later, the phone on his desk trilled. Sighing, he picked it up and put it up to his ear.

"Where are you?" Maxine demanded. "I made coffee. What the hell is happening? Do you need me to come down there and handle it?"

Sam closed his eyes. He could definitely use coffee, but he was in no shape to deal with his stepmother. Not now.

"No... no, Maxine. I got this. Just a problem with one of the doors."

"Did Jackson do something stupid? God dammit, you have to fire him. We can do his job easily, and we'd save his salary. He's a moron."

"Okay, Maxine, but I gotta go. I'll be up in a bit."

"Well, hurry up. I made coffee. And don't forget we're going to your sister's for lunch. You need time to get ready. I want you to look nice, for once."

Sam ended the call.

Instead of standing up and doing... something, anything, he stayed seated, staring at the grainy image of the corridor outside unit A24.

He was getting an idea. A terrible, horrible, awful, wonderful idea.

Sam picked up the handset and took a deep breath. "Come on, big guy," he said. "You can do this." He took another breath, let it out, and punched in a number.

His stepmother answered immediately.

"What is it now?"

"Hey Maxine, I need you to come down here. Something's happened."

"What is it? What did—"

"Look, just get down here. I need your help."

"What is it? I made coffee, you know. What happened?"

"Look, I don't want to say too much, but," He paused for dramatic effect. "It involves money."

Her voice was much quieter. "Money? How much money?"

"A lot. A lot of money."

He listened, but she was silent for a long time. "Is it one of the units? I knew it."

"It's in a unit that defaulted."

Again, silence from her end. Then, "How much money?"

He closed his eyes and balled his free hand into a fist in frustration. "A lot."

"Does Jackson know?"

He licked his lips and ran a hand over his face.

"No, he... uh... went home."

He glanced up at the monitor at the door hiding the horror.

"And how much money is it? It will take me a minute to get ready. I just made coffee, you know."

He closed his eyes and inhaled, and then let out a breath.

"A lot. Just get down here."

"Fine, just let me get decent. It's not easy for an old lady like me to do so much in the morning."

He listened, nodded.

"Okay. See you then."

Sam hung up and looked at the monitor again. Nothing had changed. The door remained closed. He closed the camera view.

Sam stood outside the A unit, waiting for his stepmother. He wanted her to hurry; the longer he waited, the more things could go wrong, the more regret and doubt filled his head.

He heard her before he saw her. She huffed and wheezed when she walked, partially because she rarely left their apartment, and partially because she was asthmatic, had diabetes, and was about one hundred pounds overweight. She stood beside him, wearing a housecoat and breathing hard, leaning against the door.

"Okay," she said. "So where is it?"

He nodded toward the unit. "Inside."

She tugged the door open and rumbled past him, letting the door close behind her. Sam shook his head and followed.

"What unit is it?" she said, making her way down the corridor, looking at the unit numbers.

"Just wait a second," Sam said. "I have to tell you something first."

"What is it," Maxine said. "Hurry up. I still need to take a shower. Which one is it?"

He gestured at A24. She moved to it and leaned down and tugged at the handle. "Is it locked?" She had neglected to slide the bolt free, which kept the door from moving up, but Sam didn't correct her.

He said, "Just stop, okay. I need to tell you something."

She ignored him and continued to pull at the door, doing nothing more than rattling it and tiring herself out. "This fucking thing is broken."

He went to her and grasped her shoulders and turned her around. He looked at her. "There's something bad in there."

Her piggish eyes narrowed. "Is it porn? Did you find a porn stash?"

He shook his head. "No, it's not porn. There's... there's a body in there. A dead body."

"What?" She looked from him to the closed unit. "A body? Whose body?"

"Well, there's two bodies, actually," he said. "I don't want you to freak out when we open the door and you see them."

"Two bodies? Are they gross?" She lowered her voice. "Does it stink?" *Not even worried about whose bodies they were*, Sam noted.

"Not really," he said truthfully. The mummy was too

dried to stink, and Jackson probably hadn't been dead long enough yet.

"I can handle a dead body," she said. "I found your father, remember?" Sam's father had a heart attack while on the toilet. She had found him, and then called Sam, hysterical. He was the one who called 911, and then driven three hours to console her. She couldn't handle that dead body, but... okay.

"All right," he said, and bent over and shot the bolt free, then grasped the handle and pulled the door up.

They stood together, staring, as the echoes of the opened door rattled through the building.

She stiffened and grasped his upper arm, her nails digging into his flesh. She hissed in his ear. "Is that Jackson?"

Sam nodded. "Yeah. That's Jackson."

She pulled away and looked up at him. "Did you do it?"

"What? Did I—No! Of course not! How could you ask that?"

"Then what happened to him? He's all... bloody."

Sam had prepared for this. "I think he had a heart attack or something. He was carrying a box full of empty bottles, and he fell down on top of them. They must have cut into him. I put him in here because I was so scared, I didn't know what to do."

He felt, rather than saw her glance at him. Only an idiot would believe that story. He hoped her greed outweighed her sensibility.

"What's that next to him? Is that a person?"

"It is," Sam said, "See that box it's holding? Jackson said he thought there was gold in it."

She stepped forward. "Gold? Why did he think that?"

"I don't know. I think he looked at the box before I got here, and then put it back. He was trying to keep it a secret."

She motioned at the body. "So get it. Let's open it."

Sam did his best to look forlorn. "I can't—it's too much. It creeps me out."

"Sam, come on, pull yourself together," she said.

"I can't," he said, backing away.

She shook her head in disgust. "Unbelievable. You're weak, just like your father."

She strode forward, clutching the front of her dressing gown together, and breathing heavily, leaned down and plucked the box from the grasp of the dead, withered hands. She nearly lost her balance when she stood up, and if Sam hadn't grabbed her meaty arm to steady her, she might have toppled over on top of both Jackson and the mummy. She shrugged out his grasp and stepped into the corridor. Her greedy fingers scrabbled to open the box. When the lid popped up, she gasped.

"Oh my God," she said.

Behind her, the mummy sat up.

"We're going to be rich," she said. But quietly. More to herself than him.

Sam moved away from his stepmother.

Behind her, there was more movement. The mummy was now on its feet, and Jackson was slowly, unsteadily, getting to his hands and knees. Sam's eyes darted from his step-mom, to the box, then the mummy and Jackson.

"So pretty," Maxine said, the glittering coins and jewels reflected in her eyes. She reached into the box and held up one of the emeralds and cooed with delight. The mummy was right behind her.

She turned to say something to Sam when a skeletal hand clamped on her shoulder. Before she could scream, before she could react, Sam moved. He snatched the box from her with one hand, sending coins and green stones flying, and he planted his other hand in the middle of her ample chest and, pistoning his legs, shoved her back, into the mummy, into the storage unit. Her arms pinwheeled and she cried out as she fell onto her back, crushing the mummy beneath her with an audible snapping. Jackson struggled to rise, apparently still getting used to his new state of being.

Sam reached up with his free hand and yanked the sliding door down, nearly dislocating his shoulder in the process. The door slammed to the floor, and moving swiftly, he pushed the sliding bolt into the receptacle. Placing the box on the floor, he reached into his pockets and pulled out the two padlocks. Hands working furiously, he double-locked the sliding bolt in place.

It wasn't until he picked up the box that his mind registered the screaming coming from inside the unit. As he went around, picking up the scattered gemstones

and coins, the screaming abated. By the time he had finished, it was quiet behind the door. Sam headed for the exit.

He sat at the computer, researching the value of emeralds. They were actually rarer and more expensive than diamonds. The small wooden box was nestled securely in his lap. In the lower right corner of the screen, a small window showed the darkened corridor outside unit A24. The audio was turned way up. A hollow, rhythmic pounding came from the tinny computer speakers. It started about ten minutes ago. Occasionally the metal door would shake with a particularly heavy blow. Staring at the screen, Sam ran a hand over his mouth. This was unsustainable. At some point, someone would hear that pounding. He couldn't keep the tenants out of Building A forever.

The storage center had opened on time that morning. The only issue, for a few early arriving renters, was that Building A was closed, apparently due to "Electrical Problems," as the sign said.

Sam opened the box for what must have been the fiftieth time and stared down at the iridescent emeralds and gold coins. He picked up a silver bracelet, festooned with small red stones, and held it up to the window. He twisted his fingers, watching as the glittering gems caught the light.

Bang! Bang!

He nearly dropped the bracelet, but he managed to place it back in the box. He glanced at the screen, thinking that the mummy had finally broken out, but the door still held.

Bang! Bang! Bang!

Sam looked over the top of the monitor at the office door. Behind the shade, someone was standing there. An impatient somebody, apparently, as he knocked again, three machine gun blasts on the wooden door.

"Okay, okay," Sam said, sliding the wooden box into a desk drawer and clicking off the monitor. He moved to the door and slid aside the shade. His heart was pounding. Had somebody called the cops? He let out a breath he hadn't realized he'd been holding when he saw that it was Carl. Carl was a tenant, an old guy who smelled like cigarette smoke and who liked to spend all Saturday in his unit, reorganizing his boxes, restacking furniture, going through his stuff... he never brought anything in, and he never took anything with him when he left. Maxine hated him, thought he was a creep, hiding kiddie porn or something in his storage unit. Sam didn't mind him. He just liked to be around his stuff, which Sam realized with mounting terror, was in Building A.

Sam unbolted the door and opened it just enough to speak.

"What the hell's going on?" Carl said. "Why's the door locked?"

He leaned into the door, and Sam had to put his weight against it to keep it closed.

"We have a problem in Building A," Sam said. "Can't let anyone in until... uh... an electrician gives the okay."

"I don't need electricity," Carl said. "I got a flashlight."

"There's uhh... danger of a fire," Sam said. "Burnt wires, stuff like that."

Carl backed off a little, but he was still annoyed. "Well how long is that gonna take? I need to get into my space."

Sam shook his head, letting Carl know he understood the inconvenience. "I'm not sure. Probably not until this afternoon. Maybe come back tomorrow?"

Behind him, the banging continued. He had turned off the monitor but the computer speakers were still on.

"Look," he said, "I'm on the phone right now with the electrician. The sooner I can get back to him, the sooner I can open your unit. Okay?"

Carl thought about this, scratched his head, nodded, and left. Sam shut the door and locked it. This wouldn't last. He had to do something. The way he saw it, he had two options; go back into Building A and kill the mummy, Jackson, and Maxine. Then he needed to dispose of the bodies and clean up. All during broad daylight.

Option two was to run.

Five minutes later, he was in his bedroom, throwing clothes into an open suitcase on his bed. The wooden box sat beside the suitcase. He hurried to the bathroom, scooped up his toilet kit and anything he could carry, and dumped it into his suitcase.

He wasn't sure where he was going, but he couldn't stay here. Someone would eventually open up that unit. And then what? A living dead mummy? Would it be in the newspapers? They'd be looking for him. Sam went into Maxine's bedroom and gazed over the heaps of unfolded clothing, delivery boxes of weight loss products, and unused exercise equipment until he saw her purse. He grabbed her wallet and pulled out all the cash. His heart sank. Only about sixty bucks. He pocketed the rings from her dresser and then grabbed her car keys.

Sam had a passport from a trip to Costa Rica they'd taken about four years ago, and he tossed it in his suitcase. Maybe he could go back to Costa Rica. American money went far there. He could sell off the jewels a little at a time, just enough to avoid suspicion, and live like a king. Maybe open a cafe or something. For the first time in what felt like years, he spied a little hope. Maybe this was for the best. He could wipe the computers clean, take away anything that showed he worked there. Of course, his fingerprints were everywhere, if it came to that, but he *had* worked there, after all. His fingerprints should be all over.

Wheeling his suitcase behind him, he hurried back to the office. He glanced briefly at Building A, but only for a moment. Yep, still there. If he had looked closer, he would have noticed that the door was ajar.

In the office, he went to the filing cabinet and removed his employee file and put it in the outside pocket of his suitcase. He opened the floor safe and took out the small blue money box. There was a few hundred dollars in there, along with the company credit card. He wouldn't use that unless he absolutely had to. He'd watched enough cop shows to know they could trace you by following your credit card trail.

He went to the computer and unplugged the external hard drive, which joined the credit card in his suitcase. He stood and looked around. Outside, a car door slammed. Instinctively, Sam ducked below the window sill. He listened. He had seen a couple of cars parked beside Building B, so maybe it was one of them. He relaxed and stood up.

"Okay," he said to nobody in particular. "Let's do this." He reached for the doorknob when the door burst open, cracking him against his fingers and smashing his knuckles.

Sam cried out in pain and brought his injured hand to his chest. When he looked up, he forgot about his pain.

The mummy stood in the doorway, holding its knife. Behind it was Maxine and Jackson.

The three of them crowded through the door and Sam backed up.

Someone will see them, thought Sam. It's going to be okay.

The mummy slashed out with the knife but Sam instinctively held up his suitcase. The knife stabbed into it. The mummy pulled at it, but once again it was stuck. Gazing at Sam with its blazing, hate-filled eyes, it released the knife and grasped either side of Sam's head. Sam froze, still holding the suitcase in front of him. The mummy pressed its hands against the sides of Sam's head, squeezing it. He dropped the suitcase and reached up, grabbing the mummy's wrist. They were so frail and thin, almost child-like, but he was unable to twist them away from his head. A white pain surged through his skull, and he felt something snap behind his left eye. Blood trickled out of his nose.

Jackson reached out and tugged at one of Sam's arms,

pulling it away from the mummy. Maxine clawed at his other arm. Sam fell back against a wall. A picture fell, hit his shoulder, and crashed to the floor. He had nowhere to go. Maxine was on his side, her cold, dead face right up next to him.

The last sound he heard was a loud crack and then everything went dark.

Sam was at peace. All was well. The treasure was safe. Along with Ekkekkeko the Guardian and the others, he would protect the royal treasure from infidels and intruders. He too, was a guardian. He finally had a purpose.

ABOUT THE AUTHOR

For more from our great authors please visit www. DumblebeeBooks.com. We hope you have enjoyed this book and encourage you to leave a review.

Visit the authors of this book at:
Mercedes M. Yardley
https://mercedesmyardley.com/
Jeff Strand
https://jeffstrand.wordpress.com/
Tim Waggoner
https://www.timwaggoner.com/
Mathew Kaufman
https://www.mathewkaufman.com/

www.ingramcontent.com/pod-product-compliance
Lightning Source LLC
Chambersburg PA
CBHW071925220626
47052CB00002B/456